To Kathleen —
Enjoy!

Copyright © 2012 Evie Maxfield
Cover art and interior layout by Clint Irwin
Author photo, Joe Tom Collins

For Mom, who else?

Tasteless

72 Steps	7
Sex and Death	21
The Surge	33
Googem	47
Gracie and Other Undesirables	61
A Night Out With the Chickens	75
The Cooking Lesson	89
Olympic Fever	101
Waiting For Bunnies	113
Tasteless	131
Bishop Desmond Tutu, the Runt of the Litter	145
My Better Half	172

72 Steps

I clearly remember my mother hollering out the back door, interrupting a perfectly good summer afternoon. I was in the middle of an enthusiastic push, flinging my kid brother skyward on the leather strop that squashed his diapered bottom. Greg screamed gleefully, clutching the rusty chains for dear life as the rickety three legged death trap that passed for a swing set teetered near collapse. I considered sending him over the top, but it just wasn't worth the trouble I'd get in. She called for us again, telling us it was time to pack. My mother was excited to be moving out of suburbia and back to her home turf, a mysterious place called The Bronx, but I was not so convinced it was a good idea. I looked longingly at the swing set, Greg still rocketing like a little human pendulum, and then at the enormous airfield behind our fenced in yard. Yet another Grumman's plane was fast making its way down the runway towards our house, and at the last possible moment, it lifted up, passing over our heads, rendering us temporarily deaf. "Epwain!" Greg squealed above the roar, his lips stained orange from the rust he'd licked off his fingers. "Yep, airplane," I agreed, already missing the constant fly-bys and the painful ringing they left in my head.

We didn't have much to pack, my mother, brother and I. A box of Hefty bags did the trick, and everything else got left behind. My mother believed in travelling light, claiming we had Gypsy blood and needed to move around a lot, but I knew she was just bored. I'd heard tales of her wild city childhood, and I tried to imagine myself tough and fearless, wearing lipstick and smoking cigarettes just like her. We took a cab into the city, all the Hefty bags stuffed in the trunk, and I had time to imagine what my new life would be like. Goodbye, boring old suburbs! I tried to convince myself that I was happy to leave it all behind. I'm a city girl now, I thought, as I bit my nails down to the quick.

The cab ride from Long Island to the big city took only an hour, but I felt like we'd travelled to the other side of the world. My mother herded us out of the cab, and I stared in awe at the monolithic brick building that was to be our new home. "This is what's known as a Pre-war Tenement", my mother explained. "Wow! A Pre-war Tenement!" I repeated. I had no idea what it meant, but it sounded exciting, like we were moving into the Museum of Natural History. I would soon discover that pre-war described the lack of many modern conveniences, like an elevator and a functioning heating system. But at that moment my excitement was fresh, and this vision of grandeur took my breath away. My mother lifted Greg to her hip, and we stepped inside the cavernous entryway. It was meat locker cold, even on this hot summer day, and it took my eyes a moment to adjust to the gloom. I looked up at the ancient, dust-covered chandelier where tiny orange light bulbs cast a pitiful glow, turning the hallway a strange mustard hue. It made us all look like we'd been prematurely embalmed, and I decided it would be fun living in a house that looked like Count Dracula's castle.

Up the stairs from the grand entrance were five apartments lined up like jail cells, all lit up by a bare 25 watt light bulb. The hallway smelled like Lysol and cabbage, the source of which was the ancient inhabitants living behind those doors. Over the years, I would become quite familiar with all the octogenarians and the sauerkraut cooking smells that belched forth from their apartments, and I tried my hardest to avoid them, but Mrs. Gottbaum, who was deaf as a post somehow sensed when I was trying to sneak past her door. She would open it a crack just as I tip toed past, and beckon me closer with her crooked, stick like finger, and then hand me a tiny, tidy garbage bag and a penny. I didn't mind taking out her trash, but I dreaded the times she invited me in for a Matzoh with oleo. Then I would have to sit politely at her little Formica table, listening to the blaring television and catching whiffs of her pot of boiling fart soup. I knew that Mrs. Gottbaum was just a sweet, lonely old lady, but I really resented the penny. What did she think I could do with it? Unless I had another penny, I couldn't even buy a piece of Bazooka gum. On my way out, Mrs. Gottbaum would pat my head with her bony little hand and say "Thank you, Wilhelm!" Not wanting to offend, I would smile back at her and say, "You're welcome."

I also learned to steer clear of apartment 1B, where the dreaded Mr. Lipshitz lived. Poor Mr. Lipshitz always had something leaking from his face. He was so ancient that he'd lost the ability to contain any of his body fluids. Sometimes I was unlucky enough to get stuck behind him in the hallway and I would need to carefully dodge the moist trail he left on the tile floor on his painfully slow shuffle to schul. Mr. Lipshitz wore a Depression era suit and hat, relics from a time when he was obviously a more robust guy. Awash in his own fluids, he drifted down Cruger Avenue, kept afloat by the enormous folds and flaps of his ancient suit. The neighborhood kids made cruel comments, like "Mr. Lipshitz on the bus!" but he never heard the taunting, thanks to the over sized Fedora that fell below his ears.

On the day I took my maiden walk down that dark hallway, I was blissfully ignorant of these tenants and their advanced states of decrepitude, and I imagined that behind every door was a young, happy family full of eager, friendly kids my age just waiting to share their bounty of toys. My mother ushered us towards the staircase. "OK, kids, let's go. Apartment 4A" she said. I looked up at the imposing marble steps. Apartment 4A meant we were on the 4th floor, and we began our ascent, placing our feet in the worn smooth spots, just like the thousands of families before us. As my hand glided along the rough, wrought iron banister, I counted each step. Twelve to the landing, where an enormous, grime encrusted window gave us a panoramic view of the alleyway with its splendid wealth of garbage cans, and then another twelve to the next floor, giving us an exhausting seventy two step climb to our apartment, a journey I would come to know and loathe through the years. I learned to trick myself into thinking the climb was actually much shorter by taking two or even three steps at a time, straining my hamstrings to their limits. I endeavored to make the trip down the stairs just as challenging, vaulting down as many steps as I could without snapping my anklebones. The fun was in seeing how fast I could make it from the apartment door to the outside stoop. My personal best was 16 seconds, but that was the time I fell down the last flight, so it didn't actually count.

Gasping for breath, we arrived on the fourth floor. My mother took a moment to light a cigarette and replenish her straining lungs with invigorating nicotine. Greg, still balanced on her hip, smacked the door with his soggy palm, leaning in closer to lick the peep hole. "Yes, I know, Greg wants to go inside" my mother said, and she dug out the key from her beaded purse. We entered the apartment through the vast, sunny kitchen where towering cabinets scraped the ceiling, rendering them inaccessible to normal sized humans who weren't blessed with orangutan arms. The lowest one was well over my mother's head and it was impossible to reach the middle shelf without an extension ladder. Any food product unlucky enough to get stored up there was immediately forgotten about, and there it would molder for eternity.

My favorite part of the kitchen was an unusual built in cabinet that would come to be known as The Toy Closet. Although it was a closet in the conventional sense, it had no door, no shelves, and no bar for hangers, but it did have a half wall blocking the entrance, so if you needed to store something, you simply flung it in. The closet was so deep, you couldn't see all the way into the back. It was the black hole of storage, and it became a catch-all for everything from coats, sweaters and scarves to broken appliances, old paint cans, construction material, furniture and the occasional bag of garbage. The only time we ever cleaned out The Toy Closet was when my mother was desperate for the spare change that could be found under the tonnage. One brave soul would have to venture into the closet and unload its contents without becoming trapped or maimed by falling debris. One time our cat went missing for a week. We thought she'd somehow gotten out, but it turned out she was hiding in The Toy Closet, living off all the Spam dinners my brother and I had ditched into it. She came out plump and healthy, with a lustrous shine to her coat.

It didn't take us long to settle into the three room apartment. The living room doubled as my mother's bedroom, and my brother and I shared the small back room. At first I felt unnerved by the tiny space, the lack of a back door, no access to a yard, but I would soon discover there was much fun to be had in a fourth floor apartment for kids unaccustomed to such a grand view. One of our windows looked out over the alleyway, and my brother immediately discovered the joys of tossing things out of it. He was fond of hearing my books smash against the garbage cans below, and giggled as he watched my sweaters and underwear flutter gently to the ground. I worked diligently to intimidate Greg, employing subtle psychological warfare in an effort to make him stop. When my mother wasn't watching, I would whisper in his ear, "I'm going to hurt you as soon as mom goes to the store," and "Mom is going to leave you at Mr. Lipshitz's house to live forever," but Greg would not be denied his fun, and the flinging continued as did my threats of pain and abandonment. Eventually, my mother solved the problem by nailing the window shut.

The other window in our bedroom opened onto a fire escape, and faced busy White Plains Road and the number two elevated train line. We were so close to the "el", it sounded like the train was pulling right into the apartment. We quickly grew accustomed to the scream of grinding wheels and hissing hydraulics, and missing every punch line on Laugh-In, but we found other ways to keep ourselves amused. During the commercial breaks, Greg would run to the window and holler things to people getting off the trains. "Help!" was one of his favorites, and certainly got the most enthusiastic response from the tired commuters. He also liked to yell "Taxi!" and this was usually followed by the sound of screeching tires from the street below.

We had no furniture at first, save for a couple of beds and a prehistoric console TV set, and my mother decided to give the place a mod, hippie feel by hanging beaded curtains and painting it a shocking variety of colors. Cobalt blue was the color she chose for the bathroom, and mid way through, she got bored of painting and left the open can on the bathroom floor. Seeing a grand opportunity for fun, my brother spilled the paint and placed our Siamese cat in the puddle. Py left a trail of little blue cat prints on the bathtub, sink and toilet, across the floor and then through the bedroom, finally ending up on the window sill.

My mother decided she liked the novelty of it, and left the prints, which were a good source of conversation when guests came by.

Greg realized bathrooms were a great untapped source of amusement after that. He especially liked to harass me when I needed to have a little private time, and he would hover outside the bathroom door. I could hear his noisy breathing as he pressed his face close to the door jamb.

"Evie poopin?" he would ask.

"Get away from the door!" I would scream.

"Evie poopin! Evie poopin!" he would shout, and then he would run to the bedroom window and announce it to the riders waiting on the subway platform.

Greg became overly fond of putting things in the toilet. He liked to watch as his Matchbox cars swirled in the rush of flushing water, and his favorite comic books swelled to epic proportions, making Superman's muscles even more impressive. One time the toilet became so clogged, my mother had to break down and call the building super to come up and look at it. Greg watched proudly as the super snaked out seventeen potatoes and a jump rope. After that, my mother stopped buying small, round vegetables and suggested I learn how to ride a bike.

Countless times I traversed those four flights up and down from our apartment. I came to know every crack and stain in the tiles, every smooth spot worn in the stairs, which families made the most noise and the worst smells. But the two flights above us remained a dark mystery, as uncharted as the far reaches of outer space. Up on the sixth floor was a fire escape style ladder leading to the roof, and my mother made it abundantly clear that if we were foolish enough to venture up there, we would experience nose bleeds, vertigo, and disorientation so violent that we would be uncontrollably drawn to the edge of the roof and plunge to our deaths.

As if that wasn't enough to crush all thoughts of roof top adventures, there was also the Krantz family on the 6th floor. I dreaded the Krantz family more than the six story plunge. Mrs. Krantz was built like a cube, five feet tall and as wide as a doorway, with the musculature of a circus strong man. She had a voice like a wood chipper, so harsh and grating that even a pleasant exchange like "Hi, how are you?" could leave you with a tooth ache for the rest of the day. When she screamed out the window for their youngest son Marvin to come in for lunch, kids all over the neighborhood would run for cover, holding their ears in agony. Marvin went to great lengths to avoid his mother, hiding under cars or up on the forbidden roof for hours, and many pleasant summer afternoons were ruined for the local children as they abandoned their Barbie dolls and stickball games to escape Mrs. Krantz's bellowing. In stark contrast to the family matriarch was Mr. Krantz, a gangly, towering stick figure of a man. He sported an enormous walrus moustache, and when he spoke, which was not often, the words came out in a muffled expulsion of air, like his lips were being sucked off his face by a vacuum cleaner. As if in defiance of all the laws of natural selection, they managed to produce three children, the youngest being the aforementioned Marvin. Marvin spoke in grunts, squeaks and whistles, and would play in places no other children dared to go, like behind the garbage cans in the alley, or in the tall weeds of the glass strewn vacant lot. He and my brother were the same age, but Greg would only play with him out of desperation. Sometimes Marvin would coerce Greg into going up on the roof with him. Greg would stand by and watch as Marvin hocked gobs of spit which floated gently down onto the people walking by six stories below. Marvin would scream with delight and motion my brother over to join in the fun, but Greg would politely decline, claiming to have a busy afternoon of vandalizing mailboxes, and then make his way nervously down the fire escape ladder before running home to vomit up his lunch.

The middle Krantz child was Johna, who was five years older than me. Although lucky enough to resemble neither of her parents, she was still disturbingly unattractive, a fact which didn't seem to bother her endless stream of eager suitors. Johna's favorite place to hang out with her boyfriends was under the stairwell, and I would try to race past without hearing the wet smacking sounds they made. Sometimes Johna would corner me later in the day to tell me all about how she and her latest boyfriend had a "make out session." "Do you like to make out?" she would enquire, while snapping her gum and readjusting her bra strap, and I would nod knowingly. "Sure. Who doesn't?" I would say, trying to sound casual. But I had no idea what she was talking about, and these conversations always left me feeling a little dirty and ashamed. My mother called her "loose." She also called her "the milkman's kid," which I thought meant she had farm-fresh skin.

Lance was the eldest, and by far, the most menacing of the Krantz kids. Lance would loiter in the doorway with his gang of sullen friends, smoking and spitting, and making it awkward for anyone to pass. I sensed that he was actually one of those sensitive if misunderstood guys. I formed this opinion the day he held the door open for me and my mother. While all his friends gave unsolicited opinions of my mother's butt, Lance gallantly stepped aside, and in a gentlemanly fashion asked my mother if she wanted to see his package. I was excited, curious to find out what might be in the package, maybe a toy or some candy! But my mother rudely ignored his offer, much to my disappointment. Feeling embarrassed by my mother's lack of manners, I asked him if maybe he could save the package for me, which all his friends found hilarious, and caused my mother to grab me by the arm and drag me up the stairs.

Living on the fourth floor came with a unique set of challenges, such as getting the groceries up the stairs. This was not a problem for my mother. She believed in buying food on a "need to eat" basis, as menu planning smacked of domesticity, which she said was for fancy people, and I would get sent to the store according to my mother's whims fifteen to twenty times a day.

"Quick, run to Mr. Levy's store and get three slices of American cheese. Hurry!" My mother would hand me a dime and push me out the door. I would bring back the emergency cheese, and she would be waiting for me with a handful of pennies. "Here, go over to Shmerle's and buy me a can of peaches. And don't dawdle!" Racing back with the precious fruit, my mother would announce that we had run out toilet paper, and send me to old Anna's with a quarter, which bought one roll. All the shopkeepers would treat me with disdain, as if it was an inconvenience to ring up a single item. "Whadya mean, three slices of American cheese? Who buys three slices of American cheese? Buy a half a pound, already!" Mr. Levy would complain. I tried to imagine Mr. Levy naked, standing there at the slicer with his fat tushy hanging out for all the world to see, so he would know how it felt to be humiliated. This didn't make me feel any better, and every time I shopped at his store, I suffered an attack of embarrassment for having envisioned him naked.

Aside from the minute by minute pilgrimages to the grocery store, laundry day was the event I dreaded the most. This rare occurrence came only when the very last pair of pants was so dirty that it could stand in the corner all by itself. My mother would stuff every available pillow case to the brim, and pile them all onto my brother's stroller. Although you might think it would be easy for a seventy pound nine year old to navigate this load down four flights of stairs, three hundred pounds of filthy clothes on wheels can really fly once it gets going. Nine times out of ten, the tiny stroller would go careening down to the landing below, where it would land in a Technicolor heap of stiff socks and mildewy towels. Having survived the descent, doing the laundry was easy. My method was this: smash all I could into a single, institutional sized washing machine, feed it the required amount of quarters, and then spend all the money I had saved by using one machine instead of three at the candy store. Sucking on Lik-m-ades made the time fly while I waited for the wash to finish, and once again, using my cost effective method of crushing it all into a single dryer, I would work my way through a sack full of jaw breakers while watching the over filled machine dry the load in a mere four hours. Once back home, I would empty the crammed pillowcases onto the floor, the still hot clothes looking like they'd just come out of a trash compactor. My mother and I would spend the evening in front of the TV set, watching our favorite shows, and pounding the hardened blocks of cloth back into the shapes of tee shirts and dungarees.

As exciting as it sounds, it was a Spartan existence we had there in apartment 4A. My mother eschewed many of the creature comforts some might consider necessary for civilized living, such as dishes, which she frowned upon as elitist. "What's wrong with eating out of the pot?" she would argue. "That's what people did for thousands of years, before they invented paper plates." Her forays into the culinary arts were rare, which worked out just fine, considering every time she decided to cook, she had to borrow a pot from a neighbor. It was usually the kind covered in dents, permanently burned on the bottom, and lacking anything that might reasonably be called a handle. Using someone else's abused cookware gave my mother a sense of entitlement, and she never felt bad about shoving the pot, full of leftover spaghetti, into the deepest recesses of the refrigerator, where it would be forgotten and eventually engulfed in mold. When the stink of rancid pasta and penicillin grew overwhelming, she would throw the pot in the garbage, indignant at the thought of having to wash anything so foul.

Given her aversion to tradition and domesticity, it's safe to say my mother lacked even the most basic knowledge of food and how to prepare it. This dearth of culinary savvy extended even to using the simplest of tools. It wasn't unusual to see my mother eating ice cream with tweezers, or stirring her instant coffee with a curtain rod. I'd seen her feed my brother baby food with a steak knife, and butter toast with a nail file. Although we were always encouraged to drink juice straight from the carton, we did own one Welch's jelly glass, which we called "The Guest Glass," and my mother's favorite day-glo orange tin cup, which kept her coffee exceptionally hot but left painful welts on her fingers and lips. She didn't really seem to mind.

Every once in a while my mother went on a cleaning spree, and one fine, hot summer day, she ventured to empty the refrigerator of its moldering contents, which included the remnants of Christmas dinner and a hairy orange. She had me bring the bag of reeking garbage down to the alleyway, making it my twenty third round trip of the day in the blistering summer heat. I struggled back up the four flights, sweating and gasping for air, and as I made my way to the refrigerator for a cold beverage, I noticed the Welch's jelly glass on the table, full of icy Kool-Ade. Next to it was a neatly folded napkin.

"Are we having company?" I asked my mother, bewildered.

"No, that's for you" she said. I looked at her in disbelief, and felt such a sense of overwhelming gratitude that I had the urge to run to her and loose myself in a motherly embrace. But in the next instant I felt embarrassed, so I picked up the glass and downed the refreshing grape drink, and then dabbed at my lips with the perfectly triangular napkin.

"All done?" she asked. I nodded, and she motioned me over with a jerk of her head. Here it comes, I thought, and I felt joy, and a pure happiness that I lived in a world where mothers poured glasses of juice for their daughters, and folded napkins, and expressed their feelings with warm hugs. I walked up to my mother, and reaching out, she pushed a dollar bill into my clammy hand.

"Here" she said. "Go buy me a pack of cigarettes. And hurry it up."

Sex and Death

After several days of being holed up in my sweltering little bedroom, I tired of watching my brother coerce all the tiny pieces from my board games through the fire-escape slats and could no longer come up with any new threats that would produce even the mildest anxiety.

"Stop it!" I yelled over and over, and Greg would cheerfully slide another Monopoly figurine over the edge to the vacant lot below.

"Mom! Make him stop!" I whined.

"That's it. Go outside and make some friends" she demanded. I dreaded this moment. I could hear all the kids outside, screaming and laughing, playing their city games. I knew I would have to go down there and brave it. I'd faced down girlie cliques before, and bribed my way into many inner sanctums with a choice Barbie or a baby doll. But having lived a relatively male-free existence, I had no idea how to be around boys. To me, they were a strange species inhabiting a foreign world, as unknowable as tube worms on the abyssal plain.

Admittedly, my experiences with the opposite sex were limited. There was my vigorous and practiced loathing of my kid brother, but to be fair, he barely fit the definition of "male". Sure, he had a penis, as I discovered the day

I caught him peeing on my dresser, but in every other respect, he was less like a boy and more like a strange species from a distant planet. Unlike the boisterous boys on the block, Greg was not just quiet, he barely spoke at all. While other boys were outside, tossing a ball around in the sunshine and fresh air, Greg would sequester himself inside, playing in his "office," an old Samsonite suitcase where he kept a constantly-updated collection of the New York Times, world atlases, instructional manuals, college textbooks and foreign language tapes, flashlights, batteries, tins of Spam, a set of tiny screwdrivers, petroleum jelly, and a toothbrush. At the age of four, Greg seemed to be preparing for Armageddon, while honing his skills as a safecracker and international spy. It was not uncommon for my mother to wake from an afternoon nap to find all the inner workings of our television set removed with surgical precision. Greg would carefully display and organize all the parts, not unlike a factory schematic, but the knobs were temptingly small and we would often have to rescue them from his cheeks. One particularly hectic day, Greg turned on all the gas jets on the stove, and then removed the knobs and cleverly hid them in his office. My mother discovered the leaking gas with Greg sitting placidly by, sucking on a razor sharp pull top from one of his cans of Spam. When he wasn't deconstructing, he was quietly building complex booby traps, usually involving twine, breakable items of great value to me, and at least one family pet. Painful experience taught me to use extreme caution when entering any room where Greg had been alone for more than ten minutes. My mother realized very early on that Greg marched to his own bizarre drummer, and it wasn't so much that he was incapable of having a normal conversation or a game of catch like a regular kid, but that he chose to put his energies into more off-beat activities, like annoying the crap out of me and planning mass global destruction.

The only other man in my life was my grandfather. Again, he was not the best example of a typical guy. For one thing, he refused to let me call him grandpa.

"You call me Ernie, just like everyone else," he instructed. "I'm no goddamn old man".

And this was true. He was a mere forty-two when I was born, and immediately thrust into the role of babysitter, as he was perpetually unemployed, and my grandmother thought this was a good way to keep him out of trouble. While most grandpas might think an afternoon in the park would be time well spent with a grandchild, Ernie preferred the cozy confines of what he playfully called "The Gin Mill." This was a mysterious place, darkly lit and smoky. It had magical signs that moved, creating a peaceful, contemplative atmosphere. One announced that Shlitz was "The Premium Beer," with swirling rainbow colors, while another had handsome clydesdale horses proudly carting their precious cargo into perpetuity. The signs seemed designed to induce a calm state of meditation, and I would sit enthralled atop my barstool, with a bowl of maraschino cherries and an endless supply of shirley temples for my lunch. Sometimes I would watch the tiny black and white TV, while Ernie palled around with his bar buddies, drinking the afternoon away. I loved our visits to the Gin Mill. Perhaps they didn't promote what most might call a normal bonding experience, like how a nice bedtime story or visit to the petting zoo might, but without fail, at the end of the day Ernie and I went home happy and very, very relaxed.

In contrast to these unusual examples of masculinity, the local boys were a feast for the senses – loud, smelly, profane and violent. I never knew such an animal existed, until that fateful July afternoon when I boldly introduced myself to a promising bunch of prospective girlfriends sitting on a nearby stoop. "If you play with me, I'll give you my Baby Brenda," was my ace in the hole. One or two girls looked up with interest, accepted my bribe, and I was in. And so I began to learn how to navigate the complex world of city kids at play. With girls, it was all about cooperation and hierarchy, who got to be the mommy or the daddy, who had the best dollhouse, and the neatest coloring books. For boys, the idea of play seemed to involve a nebulous set of rules regarding how and when to inflict pain. I settled into a stoop-side game of "I'll be the prettiest Barbie with the best clothes and the nicest car and you be Ken," with me, the new girl, in the obviously less desirable role of Ken. Out in the street, something fascinating was going on – the boys had launched into a game of Hot Peas and Butter, a testosterone driven bloodfest that was basically hide and seek with corporal punishment. One boy would hide a leather belt, while the others closed their eyes and counted to ten. Whoever found the belt got to beat their friends senseless before they made it to home base. It was an excellent spectator sport, as viewers got to witness the hiding of the belt, and then enjoy the thrilling sensation of knowing someone was going to "get it." When the boys grew bored of beatings, there was the old standby, stick ball. Although it required great amounts of athletic ability, stick ball was ultimately a game of verbal abuse and fist fights, the most extreme punishment being reserved for the kid who hit the ball into the sewer. I was in awe, watching these boys pummel their way through sleepy summer afternoons.

Eventually, like puppies, even the wildest kid would need a break from blood sport. It was around dinner time of my first day ever with my new friends when the boys dropped their sticks and belts and settled down to a nice relaxing evening of rampant cursing on the stoop. We girls were still deeply engrossed in a bitter game of "A, my name is Alice," when Linda got tripped up by the letter T. Stevie chimed in, "T, my name is Titties," which was followed by: "U, my name is Udder," and the more obvious: "V, my name is Vagina." What came next truly baffled me for a number of reasons, as Bobby sang out: "W, my name is Hoo-ah." I laughed along with the gang, but later, as we all headed towards home for dinner, I couldn't help but ponder this strange reference. First of all, was Bobby so ignorant that he didn't realize Hoo-ah started with an "H?" Second, what on earth could this Hoo-ah be? I considered asking my mother, but because the questionable word was nestled between extremely embarrassing references, including "X my name is X-ray of my ass," I hesitated to bring it up. I didn't want my friends to know how ignorant I was, so I kept it under my hat, and feigned a worldliness I surely didn't possess when it came to tawdry Bronx lingo. I stayed in the dark until several months later when a nice girl named Andrea moved into my building. She was smart and I knew she wouldn't judge me for my innocence, so when she taught me to sing "Walking down Canal Street," I asked about the part: "I couldn't find a Hoo-ah." Andrea kindly wrote it down for me. "W-H-O-R-E." Ah! At last, I understood the mystery of the disappearing "r", a mainstay of the Bronx mother tongue. I felt enlightened, able to communicate effectively with the natives. Now I was truly a Bronx kid! The next time we sang "Walking down Canal Street," it would be with conviction and joy! And Andrea, being such a patient tutor, didn't think any less of me when I asked her what a whore was.

The first night of my first day ever with my brand new friends gave me a somewhat different view on life. This was the time when every kid waited anxiously for the ice cream man to come, and the boys and girls enjoyed cooperative play together, meaning no one got intentionally injured, or called a motherless son of a bitch bastard. We all competed side by side in marathon games of stoop ball, which only required the small pink rubber ball called a "spaldeen," and the ability to count by fives into the millions.

Stoop Ball was one of those games that could go on for hours, or even days if the remaining competitors were stubborn enough to keep it going, and the spaldeen didn't end up squashed under a car. The object was simple: bounce the ball against the step and catch it. If the ball hit the back of the step, it was worth 5 points. Hit the edge, and it was 10 points. Not being a game of tremendous skill, stoop ball attracted even the kids with no athletic prowess whatsoever, including the brainiacs and the crybabies. They were the first to get eliminated, however, as dropping the ball meant instant disqualification, but for those too uncoordinated to participate in any other sport, it was a major league accomplishment just to throw the little ball once or twice and have it land miraculously in hand. I happened to be one of those kids who ducked when a moving object came hurtling towards me, but years of practice taught me that it was better to catch a projectile with my hands than the back of my head. Stoop ball was the perfect game for us non-competitive types, as there was no team to let down, no one counting on you to come through in the clutch. On the contrary, other kids were hoping you'd drop the ball, as they waited impatiently in line for their turn. I quickly learned that it was required to curse violently when your turn was over. "Son of a bitch, goddamn asshole, your mother is a hoo-ah!" was the acceptable standard. Like having a jail tattoo, cursing was a mark of experience, and earned you respect and admiration.

When everyone grew tired of stoop ball and the ice cream man had come and gone, it was time to burn off all that sugar energy, and a spooky game of nighttime hide and seek was the best way to do it. The girls tended to stick together, and pick hiding places that were fairly close by home base, whereas boys would climb trees, or crawl under cars, or even hide in dark alleyways. I found a fairly obvious, well lit front porch right across the street. Being new to the standards and practices of the game, I was unsurprised when a tough-talking ten-year-old, named Vinnie, joined me on the porch, and we hunkered down to remain out of sight. I remember being a little scared of Vinnie. He exuded a manliness the other boys lacked, which was due mostly to adolescent BO, and a liberal application of Old Spice cologne. He wore a guinea tee which showed off his burgeoning muscles and wispy puffs of armpit hair, and he already had a fuzzy shadow over his upper lip. Vinnie squatted uncomfortably close to me, his unruly mass of curly hair brushing against my face. When he casually draped his arm around my neck, I lost all the feeling in my legs, and thought I would crumple to the ground. I felt him looking at me in the dark, and the sensation was like a dentist's drill through the side of my head. What happened next is burned into my psyche like a helmet full of hot coals – Vinnie kissed me on the cheek. I felt a wave of blackness come over me, and I knew I was about to pass out. Vinnie waited for a response. I could see his teeth glowing as he smiled expectantly, and all I could do was to try not to vomit on his shoes. I have a hazy memory of standing up abruptly, mumbling "I gotta go home," and running as if my life depended on it. I could feel Vinnie watching my frantic dash, as I left the stink of fear and embarrassment behind me.

Arriving at the apartment, gasping and choking back tears, I attempted to explain to my mother what had happened. She waited patiently while I described the horror, the indignity of being kissed by a total stranger, how I felt dirty, and humiliated and confused. I didn't quite get the response I was hoping for, which was "Dear God! I will call the police right now, and we will have him arrested and put away in a jail, where he will rot until he dies." Instead, my mother lit a cigarette, and considered the extremity of my reaction. "Don't sweat the small stuff," she said.

What? What could she possibly mean by that? It was beginning to feel like a conspiracy. Everyone was in on something and I was left out in the dark, wondering about my place in the world, a world where strange boys could just fling their arms around you and breathe their Good Humor breath in your face, and plant a chocolatey kiss on you with no warning. It felt like a part of me had died, that my innocence was crushed under the weight of this hideous monster called Sex. How could I ever go outside again? Everyone would know! Like my own personal scarlet letter, Vinnie's kiss would leave a permanent brand on my cheek. I was scarred, and I knew I would never be the same.

After a night of careful consideration, I decided I didn't really need friends, and that I could be perfectly happy staying in the house for the rest of my life. This steadfast resolve wore off by about eleven the next morning, when I could hear the other kids making their way outside, riding bikes and calling each other names, living their lives as if nothing devastating had happened. I wondered if maybe Vinnie's family had suddenly decided to move away during the night, or better yet, if he'd been struck by lightning, burned to a crisp, reduced to a pile of ash and bones. By noon, I couldn't stand not knowing, and I went downstairs to find out what the repercussions were of my life-altering experience. There were my friends in their usual modes, the girls jumping rope, the boys playing King Queen against the side of the building. And there was Vinnie in the jack position, slapping the spaldeen into his neighbor's box, intent on not missing the line, and much to my amazement, not even glancing my way. I tried to act casual, like my heart wasn't pounding and my face wasn't burning hot. I joined the girls, and waited for the accusations, the sneers, the finger pointing. But again, nothing happened, except an offer to take a turn. Could it be they didn't know what happened, that my humiliation wasn't so public after all? I kept glancing over Vinnie's way, wondering when I would have to face him. I loathed the way he lunged after the ball and got it every time, the way his skinny tee shirt revealed his litheness. I felt repulsed, so why couldn't I stop looking at him? Eventually, the boys finished their game and wandered our way, and I felt myself tense up, tasted the bile rise in my throat. He was sickening, a revolting example of cockiness and ease. The boys all sat on the stoop behind us, and launched into a chorus of armpit farts, taking full advantage of their sweatiness. The laughter and the farting continued for a while, and I did my best to ignore him, desperate to not look his way. But my turn ended, and I reluctantly gave up the rope. Now was my moment of truth!

And as is the case with so many moments of truth, this one proved to be less than glorious as I discovered, there on the stoop, with his sweaty tee shirt and his furry lip, was Vinnie, sitting casually with his arm around Linda's shoulder. Linda appeared perfectly content, or at the very least, not about to barf, and I stood there, gawking. How could this be, when just the night before I was the object of his attraction? For a moment I was relieved. I was free of Vinnie's slimy bad intentions! Never again would I have to hide my face in shame, unencumbered by the crushing weight of his repulsive desires! But in the next moment, I was wracked with jealousy, and I turned and ran before anyone could see me burst into tears.

"Boys are morons," were my mother's words of comfort as she smoothed the hair against my sweaty head. I had never felt so dejected in my life. I vowed to never, ever go back outside to play, this time swearing to God, hope to die, strike me dead on the spot if I should take one step out of the door. My mother brought me an icy cold glass of Kool-Aide and put on Saturday cartoons, and I spent the rest of the day playing Matchbox cars with Greg, happy in the comfort that there was no hidden agenda between me and my brother, just pure, undisguised hatred.

That night, my mother suggested that I go outside, but I opted instead to stay in and play five card stud with her. It was a warm, humid night, and I could hear the neighborhood come alive with children laughing and shouting and the jangling music of the ice cream truck, and I felt sorely left out. I played without much conviction, and lost all my pennies after only a few games, and I went back into my room to sit in the fire-escape window. My mother joined me, and we sat there, feeling the cool breeze coming off the arriving subways. "You know, somewhere out there, right now, is the boy you are going to fall in love with and marry," she said. I looked out onto busy White Plains Road, and imagined that down there, amongst the crowds of people, was my future soulmate, perhaps enjoying an Archie comic at the newsstand, or dining on hot dogs at the kosher deli. Or better yet, maybe he was from some far off exotic land, like Queens or New Jersey! I tried to envision what he might look like. I painted a mental picture of my perfect husband: he did not have a fuzzy upper lip, and always wore a button-down shirt, and never tried to show off his stringy, muscular arms. He had shiny, straight hair, he was very clean, and wore a mod jacket, like Paul McCartney on the "Help" album. I started to imagine how dreamy it would be to marry Paul when I remembered that lately he'd been sporting an ugly moustache and wrote scary songs about walruses and egg men. I quickly erased Paul off this mental list, and penciled in Davey Jones of The Monkees. Davey was cute and non-threatening, every eight-year-old-girl's dream come true. Yes, I could picture myself with Davey, and began planning all the fun we would have playing Barbie. I knew he wouldn't mind being Ken, and I was feeling better, already.

And so it was settled. I went to bed that night with happy thoughts of Davey Jones in my mind, wondering if my mother would let him sleep on the couch after we got married, or if we should just get him a sleeping bag for the floor. I knew it really didn't matter. We would be happy together, even if he had to share the bed with Greg. I drifted off to sleep, and when I woke up the next day, I knew something was different. I felt older and wiser, and yes, I dared to think, even mature beyond my years. All worries about Vinny and my first shameful kiss had vanished, and I ran outside to play in the hot July sunshine, wondering if my friends would notice the change. I skipped down the street, humming "Cheer Up, Sleepy Jean", and hoping with every fiber of my being that this was the day I got to be Barbie.

The Surge

I was desperate to fit in, and they knew it. They could smell it on me—the freshly-cut grass, the cotton tee shirts dried in the morning sunshine; the reek of suburbia clung to me like a second skin. Years of rigorous training had enforced in me the hard-to-break habits of politeness and respect. But I was motivated to change. I watched my new friends, scrutinized their every move, and before long I was swearing with ease and fluency, stealing ice cream money from my mother's purse, laying down in the gutter on a dare. I defied, and lied, and sometimes, I spit. It felt great to be like everyone else, to fit in, to be bad, dropping Rs and acting tough, and when not within earshot of my mother, even daring to use double negatives. But every Sunday my city friends and I parted company, and I watched with envy as they all dressed up in fancy suits and frilly dresses and, glowing with holiness, paraded down to the church to confess to all the evil deeds they had committed. How I wished I had such piety! I felt a heavy guilt, the lingering taste of illicit ice cream still in my mouth. I begged my mother to let me go to church to purge myself of sin. Although not religious in any practical sense, she secretly kept holy water in an old Hellmann's jar by the side of her bed, and every so often she would take a sip, genuflect and kiss her crossed fingers, and she was spiritually good to go, having all the religious insurance she needed. "Church is for old ladies and suckers," she warned me, but I would not be deterred from what I imagined was my preordained destiny. I had this scenario in my head: I would have a spiritual awakening that was nothing short of miraculous my very first time in church, rising above the riff raff to become the most holy nine-year-old my heathen friends had ever known. Before long I would join a convent, and I imagined all the fun I would have with the other novices, sharing our humble meals, singing folk songs by the fireside. And of course, there would be the handsome Monsignor, the only man I would ever need in my life, fatherly, kind and, of course, muscular. Oh, yes. This was the life I was destined for. The following Sunday, I screwed up my courage, put on a dress, and set off on my journey to sainthood.

St. Lucy's was gorgeous and gory, with its banks of flickering votives and towering stained-glass depictions of suffering and death. At the back of the church there was an entrance to the grotto where a statue of the patron saint stood, placidly holding a small platter containing her freshly plucked eyeballs. Poor St. Lucy! I thought, my stomach lurching. She looked as casual as a hostess passing a plate of cocktail weenies. I followed my friends down the center aisle, trying not to be intimidated by the graphic portrayals of agony and horror, and I imagined that the mangled yet dashing Jesus on the cross was looking down on me with approval. I dipped my fingers into the holy water, made the sign of the cross, even pretended to know the words to the prayers and hymns. Sit, stand, kneel, genuflect, it was easy! I felt like an old pro, and I dared to think God Himself wouldn't have known I was faking it. But the sermon went on and on, and I started to drift off, fidgeting with the itchy lace collar on my dress, yawning, gawking at the bleeding, eight foot semi-naked savior, when something snapped me out of my fog—everyone was getting up and filing forwards, hands clasped in prayer, waiting to receive the tiny wafer dipped in wine. I sat, sweating in the pew, scrutinizing the crowd, trying to gauge the proper behavior. I could see the priest hold up the little white cookie thing, and my well rehearsed friends mumbled the correct response. What was it? Could I fake it? If I didn't go up, they would see right through my cheap Catholic façade! The priest would peg me for a fraud, and I would be banned from church, humiliated in front of all my genuinely religious friends. I formulated a plan, and lay down in the pew and pretended to be asleep. The gang made their way back, sucking on their holy tidbits, looking freshly blessed and self satisfied. I looked up groggily, rubbing my eyes. "Oh! Huh? Did I miss it?" I murmured, feigning disappointment, but I knew I had blown it and I felt ashamed. I sat through the rest of the sermon, bored and restless, already abandoning my hopes of ever wearing a wimple.

By the time I got home, I couldn't wait to tear off my uncomfortable dress and painful patent leather shoes. I was so happy to be out of church that I even offered to play with Greg. My mother had him perched on the kitchen table and was carefully removing pebbles from his nose with a tweezers. "So how was church?" she asked, as she extracted what looked like a fancy glass bead. "Are you going back next Sunday?" I acted very disappointed. "Nah. Father Oliveri said it was against the law to go to church without a catechism." My mother knew I had no clue what the word meant, but I'd heard my friends say it, and I knew that throwing it into my story would lend it some credibility. "That's too bad. I guess you won't be running for Pope any time soon," she said, tipping my brother's head back a little further so she could inspect his nasal cavities with a flashlight. Satisfied that my brother's nostrils were free of foreign objects, she sent me off to change out of the loathsome dress so we could head off to my grandparents' house, along with various and sundry aunts, uncles, cousins and family friends, for my grandmother's famous Sunday dinner.

For every God-fearing, red blooded Italian in New York City, Sunday meant gravy day, and it was no different for us, half-blood Italian Jew heathens though we might be, and thoughts of Googie's cooking wiped away any moral decrepitude I might still have felt in the pit of my stomach. My grandmother would slave away from the crack of dawn, preparing the gut-busting feast that was the stuff of legend in my family. My grandfather would concoct a vicious punch made from vodka, red wine and Hi-C, and the grown-ups would all get plowed and kick back while my grandmother cooked for the raucous if unhelpful crowd. Eventually, the feasting and debauchery gave way to singing folk songs, mostly old-time Woody Guthrie favorites. My grandparents, having met a million years ago at a Youth Communist League dance, still fancied themselves die-hard Reds and I suspected this was the only thing that kept Googie from killing Ernie in his sleep.

For deep down in the darkest recesses of his DNA, Ernie carried a crazy gene so potent that generations of interbreeding with "normal" people had failed to eradicate it from the pool. Its origins could be traced back to my great, great grandmother, the infamous Jenny Johnson, who mysteriously outlived seven husbands and beat her own daughter, my great grandmother, black and blue with a live chicken as my horrified grandfather looked on. This may explain why years later, permanently traumatized by the chicken beating incident, my grandfather's mother disowned him with a vigorous slap across the face for eating the last of the "gribbenis," a disgusting congealed chicken fat spread that poor immigrant Russian Jews ate, perhaps to remind themselves how terrible their lives still were, even here in the slightly less Jew-hostile New World. Ernie denied eating the stuff, despite the obvious grease smears across his cheeks. "I have no son!" she was quoted as wailing, whilst pulling out fistfuls of hair from her own head. My then fifteen year old grandfather was quite happy with the idea of being disowned, and he promptly threw away his yarmulke and devoted his life to vodka and Karl Marx.

It was just three years later that my lanky, blue-eyed Commie grandfather would Jimmy-Stewart swagger his way into my unsuspecting grandmother's heart. It was at that fateful dance where they bonded over Bolshevik banter, and before my grandmother had a chance to really think it through, they made a hasty trip to Woolworth's, where Ernie bought her a "GENUINE imitation Gold Plated Wedding Band" that would turn her finger green within twenty four hours of saying "I do." Over the next few years, my grandmother popped out a couple of kids and worked like a dog to provide for her family, while my grandfather did the one thing he was innately suited for—he went mental.

To his credit, Ernie was creative and unusually consumed by unbridled enthusiasm, and he would go on artistic rampages, spending my grandmother's hard-earned cash on photographic equipment, expensive musical instruments, wood-working saws, oil paints and canvases, model electric trains, pedigree dogs, and anything else that struck his fancy. With Googie's credit card in hand, the sky was the limit! Each new obsession would consume him for months at a time, and one by one, the rooms of their house were transformed into Ernie's private playgrounds. The bathroom became a darkroom, where an enormous enlarger blocked access to the toilet and where strange photographs of Armageddon landscapes and babies with three eyes hung from the shower curtain rod to dry. The dining room was a wood-working shop, where Googie's Depression-era glassware was perpetually covered in sawdust and creepy, headless wooden torsos leaned drunkenly against the wall like they were waiting to be frisked. Into the guestroom, Ernie crammed an enormous, pine picnic table and then spent months creating a fantastic, incredibly detailed miniature town in the Swiss Alps, where B and O model trains traversed the scenic cliffside landscapes and snow-covered hamlets that Ernie populated with tiny blonde-haired men in lederhosen. I even helped him put the finishing touches on his cozy bedroom "solarium," a peaceful wonderland of fish tanks teeming with tangs and tetras, enormous glass terrariums alive with hermit crabs and turtles, terra-cotta pots overflowing with wild and exotic flora and, of course, big, comfy chairs in which to recline and enjoy the soothing gurgles of the aerators. But as exciting and unpredictable as Ernie's imaginative outbursts were, there was always a crash waiting for him when those creative juices would just suddenly dry up. This was the time when he would withdraw into his cocoon of safety, literally wrapping himself from head to toe in a woolen blanket, with only his eyes peeking out. He could stay like this for weeks, sitting in his La-Z-Boy while his trains gathered dust, and his fish went belly up from neglect. I never questioned Ernie's erratic behavior. It was just another day in my grandparent's house, and if Ernie was "in the cocoon," Googie would simply work around him like he was some kind of lunatic flannel centerpiece.

If Ernie was riding the crest of a manic episode, it was almost impossible to get him to sit still. When he wasn't hand painting individual snowflakes on his tiny Alpine village, Ernie liked to hang out with his drinking buddies down at The Eastchester Lounge and get fall-down drunk, a pastime that occupied many of his evenings. But when a nasty late-night encounter with some concrete stairs left him with a broken nose and two black eyes, Ernie promptly gave up drinking for good. Never one to rest on his laurels, Ernie quickly filled the void with another of his favorite activities, tending his vegetable garden. It was second to none on a street full of competitive Italian gardeners, where tomato size had a directly proportionate relationship to machismo. Needless to say, the off-the-boaters hated Ernie's guts. They would come around and suspiciously gawk at his magnificent vines, where the Romas grew so plump and juicy they would drag on the ground. His zucchini were the size of baseball bats, his sugar snaps sweeter than candy. His garden was so prolific that Ernie proudly gave away bucket loads to all the envious and emasculated goombahs, if only to gloat over his bounty. "Ey!" they would accuse, "Wadda you do?" Ernie would ignore the implications that he was somehow cheating to get his veggies to perform such fantastic feats of growth. He would leave those men wondering and pitiful, ashamed of their own limp and struggling seedlings. Although he never admitted it, I knew that Ernie was venturing into his garden long after the nosy neighbors had retired, tending the tomatoes and pruning the peas, feeding, watering and weeding by moonlight. I could just picture him out there in the cool, quiet darkness, coaxing his veggies to grow with tenderness and devotion while the rest of the chaotic world slept. I'm not sure why, but those vegetables returned his love in a way that his Gin-Mill buddies never could.

Although Ernie preferred the company of his tomatoes and toy trains to that of most human beings, my grandmother always insisted that I was his favorite. This was probably true during the years when I was very small and he could bounce me on his knee as we sat perched on a bar stool, or on those tipsy drives home from the Gin Mill, when he would let me help him steer. "Don't tell anyone we played Big Girl Drives the Car today!" he would remind me, and not wanting to spoil our secret, I never did. As I got older and my perspective on things changed, I began to question not only Ernie's sanity, but why Googie put up with him all those years. Sure, they shared a love of good music and subversive politics, but even the most saintly of wives would have packed her bags and hopped a Greyhound to anywhere rather than put up with his temperamental tantrums and infuriating eating habits. Being married to one of the greatest cooks in the western hemisphere was meaningless to Ernie, and he insisted on preparing his own meals, which usually involved frying up a few slabs of salami and eating all the filling out of an Entenman's apple pie. Googie would spend days preparing her incredible homemade lasagnas, meatballs and sweet sausages, but Ernie would push his plate aside in favor of a ketchup sandwich.

My grandmother went to work every day, and paid the bills, and tended to all family matters, but it was my unstable grandfather who actually ruled the roost, if only because no one wanted to make him mad. Ernie had a notoriously bad temper, and we all tended to tip-toe around him to keep the peace. This got harder for me to do as I entered my teen years, and Ernie's fixations became more unreasonable. This was a constant source of anxiety for the whole family. "Don't be fresh to Ernie!" they would beg me. One snappy retort could send my grandfather into a month long rage, but I felt I owed it to my family to try and reason with him. One fine example of this was the day Ernie declared the use of small appliances strictly off limits, due to the dangerous electrical surges they caused. I was in the bathroom drying my hair, when Ernie pounded on the door. "What the hell is that noise?'" he demanded. "I'm drying my hair, old man!" I hollered back. Ernie stormed into the bathroom and grabbed the dryer out of my hands."No blow drier!" he barked. "You'll cause a surge!" and he yanked the cord out of the wall, leaving me with a dripping head. I complained bitterly to my mother, who was living in my grandparent's basement apartment at the time. "Look at me! I have no wings!" I shrieked. "My social life is ruined!" My mother, caught between a lunatic father with an irrational fear of electrical surges, and a hysterical, semi-coiffed teenager, advised me to buy the lowest wattage blow drier I could find at the drug store. And so, for the next few years, I used my itsy bitsy travel blow drier on the lowest, quietest setting, hiding in the basement bathroom, while my mother blasted her TV to drown out the minute electric hum. Although it would take me hours to dry my hair, my grandfather was none the wiser, peace was restored, and miraculously, my Con-Air Mini Pro never caused any deadly house fires.

Cohabitating with my grandparents had its advantages, although having a nicely coiffed hair style in a reasonable amount of time was not one of them. But for one thing, they always had a car, which was quite a luxury for city dwellers. My grandfather liked having nice things, as the indigent often do, and he had a way of convincing wary salespeople that he absolutely intended to make payments on that brand new Cadillac Coupe de Ville, and the next thing you know, he was driving it off the lot with nothing more than a winning smile and a handshake. It was great fun driving around in that boat for the two months they had it, and after it got repossessed, my grandmother insisted they downgrade to something a bit more affordable.

Not long after that, Ernie showed up at home in a 1976 electric-green Dodge Dart, quite possibly the only one of its kind, a car so hideously vibrant it could induce seizures. The salesman was only too happy to let Ernie have the car at a profoundly deep discount, just to get the thing off his lot where it was a major distraction and caused all the other, more visually pleasing cars to look bad. I learned to drive in that car, and all my friends promptly dubbed it The Erniemobile. Ernie took great pride in driving a car that was so unique. He loved ferrying my grandmother to and from the train station, where people would stare in disbelief, sometimes shielding their children's eyes. My grandparents were generous enough to let me borrow the car whenever I wanted, and every weekend, my friends and I would head out to New Jersey in it to see our favorite bands play. One night, I had the unfortunate luck of hitting a car that was pulling out of a parking space. It turned out the guy driving the car was a doctor and he didn't want the police involved, so he gave me his phone number and asked me to let him pay for the damages. The next morning, I sheepishly showed Ernie the dangling fender and the crumpled hood. I could see his face start to turn a dangerous purple color, which was even more disturbing against the backdrop of the Dodge's hideous puce, but then I showed him the crumpled note from the doctor, and explained what a nice guy he was, and how he was willing to pay out of his own pocket. The blaze in Ernie's cheeks quickly mellowed to a rosy glow, as he calculated the advantages of having the financial upper hand with a man of medicine. Ernie pocketed the note, and I never so much as got a slap on the wrist. Legend has it that Ernie met with the man at some lonely diner out on Route 46 in Totowa, where negotiations took place, and a fat manila envelope was passed under the table. As for the Dart, she drove us around for many years to come, shocking bystanders and causing temporary blindness, still sporting a dangling fender and a crumpled hood.

Through the years, my grandfather became more reclusive, angry and unreasonable, until the day he had a big-time stroke. He spent a few days in the hospital, where he mistakenly thought he was waiting to embark on a flight to Israel. He kept asking the nurses when they were going to take off, and could he please have some peanuts? The nurses humored him, and told him to fasten his seatbelt, the captain was about to announce their departure. Ernie came home a changed man. He lost his fire to create and the fear that drove him to swaddle himself in woolen insulation. Ernie was now more like a visitor in a foreign country, always a little confused, trying to find his way to the nearest train station or cafe, trying to understand a language that barely made sense. He took to hanging out down in the basement with my mother, grubbing cigarettes and beer. He would always ask her the same question, "When did you get here?" My mother would ponder for a moment, light a cigarette, and respond, "Oh, you know, the other day," and Ernie would nod, and sip his beer. They would watch a couple of game shows, and then Ernie would ask, "When are we leaving?" and my mother would say, "Ah, soon, I guess," and then Ernie would drift away back upstairs to my waiting grandmother. Ernie would announce that he was ready to go, and Googie would help him into his pajamas and put him to bed. I was a little scared of this new Ernie. He was frail and his perpetual confusion about where he was and when he was leaving put us all on edge, as if we all had somewhere to be. He would often try to leave the house, so we had to keep the doors and windows locked and barricaded. "Isn't it time?" he would argue, as he tried to remove the chair that was wedged under the doorknob. "They're all waiting!"

One day Ernie became quite agitated, and I decided to make him his favorite food, a plate of fried salami, to calm him down. I suddenly felt an awkward tenderness toward this strange man who was nothing like the explosive grandfather I once knew. I fixed him lunch, and suggested he relax in his favorite La-Z-Boy. He took the plate, sat back, and looked up at me in wonder. "Why did you do this?" he asked. I hesitated, but knowing there might not be a better opportunity, I answered, "Because I love you." Ernie looked at the dish of salami, and then back up at me. "Oh," he said. "Are you the pilot?"

My grandparents managed to stay married for 40 years, and on every anniversary, Googie put her head in her hands and moaned "Another year with the wrong man." But I would watch them together at those Sunday feasts, where the laughter and the folk songs would get the better of my grandmother and she would forgive Ernie for his wild shopping sprees, his angry rampages and irrational demands, and all the time he spent shutting her out from his quilted womb. And occasionally, their eyes would meet, and a tiny glimmer of those two idealistic teenagers would surface, and Googie would sigh and look down at her hand, twirling the dime store wedding band that still adorned her ring finger, a hastily purchased promise of better things to come.

The Surge

Googem

It couldn't have been easy for my mother, raising two kids by herself, living month to month on a meager welfare check in the gulag-like conditions of our tiny apartment. But she managed to find novel and creative ways to make life livable during even the most miserable months. On freezing winter mornings when the radiators remained cold and lifeless, she encouraged us to hammer on them to the rhythms of our favorite songs, endless fun for two bored and shivering kids, and an effective way to alert the Super to the obvious lack of heat. The sound of metal banging on metal could be heard echoing throughout the building, resounding from every apartment, in melodic contrast to the cursing and screaming of tenants as they attempted to beat some warmth out of the dormant metal relics. We were comforted by the fact that all our neighbors were miserable and angry, and that, like us, they lacked the nerve to go down and confront Mr. Lee Wong, the creepy superintendant who lived in the basement apartment down in the alley. Two things about Mr. Wong: he was a terrible superintendant, and he was most certainly not Chinese. Pale and sunken, with a greasy blonde moustache and the soulless blue eyes of a practiced assassin, he kept a smoldering cigarette glued to his lower lip, which caused him to have a permanent sneer, and when he spoke, his heavy Slavic accent cut through words like a scythe through summer wheat. My mother was convinced that he was an escapee from a Siberian prison camp, masquerading as a Chinese handyman in an attempt to hide from the KGB. During the five years that he'd been living in his Unabomberesque apartment by the garbage cans, many desperate tenants had mustered up the courage to go down and report a clogged toilet or a drippy shower, only to find the same well-weathered scrap of paper taped to his door that read "bak in 10 minit." Mr. Wong could clearly be seen through the window, watching TV in the dark and spitting into a cup, pretending not to hear the timid knocking. It's not like Mr. Wong gave the impression that he wanted to help anyone. He wore no snappy blue chambray work shirt with "Lee" embroidered over the breast pocket, neatly tucked into khaki trousers, an outfit from which one might infer the desire to be of service. No, Mr. Wong's uniform of choice was a sweat-stained guinea tee and a pair of shiny, skin-tight brown slacks, no shirt, no jacket, no socks, hairy armpits and bony ankles exposed to the world, attire which screamed, "If you bother me, I will chop you into little pieces." He could often be seen sitting on the front stoop chain smoking, his stringy, bare arms white with frost, cigarette butts gathered around his cracked, brown loafers. Maybe my mother was right, and all those years in a sub-Arctic correctional facility had rendered him impervious to frostbite and the plaintive wailings of his frozen fellow human beings. Maybe he took great joy from knowing we were all cold and miserable. Or maybe it was just an unnecessary inconvenience for him to flip the switch on the furnace. In any case, no one wanted to inconvenience Mr. Lee Wong.

And so our apartment remained heat free, and we learned to deal with the cold using more innovative techniques. One way my mother would make those subzero mornings more bearable was to crank up the oven and toss our cold-hardened dungarees into it, letting them bake until they were just about ready to burst into flames. The trick was to wriggle into them while still toasty, but not hot enough for the copper rivets to sear your flesh. She would also boil pots of water day and night, which caused the windows to form a foggy film and the floors to become slick and slippery. Despite the constant hazard of slipping and breaking a hip, we preferred the jungle like warmth over the bone jarring cold, and found that walking around with newspapers under our feet prevented unnecessary trips to the emergency room.

In the summertime, our apartment became a tiny, hot hellhole. Not a single family on all of Cruger Avenue had an air conditioner, so most people simply sat outside on their stoops with wet towels draped over their heads until the wee hours, eventually heading off to bed to lie awake in pools of their own sweat, praying for a breath of air to come in through propped-open windows. For us, hanging out on the fire escape provided much-needed breezes from the passing number-two trains, but the squeals of grinding metal combined with the fear of rolling over and dropping four stories to our deaths always drove us back to our baking bedroom. Sometimes my mother would scrape up ten cents and send me to the corner grocery for packets of Kool-Aid. But in the time it took me to drag myself to the store and back up the four flights in the oppressive heat, and then wait for my mother to stir the powdery mix in with tepid tap water, and for that gallon of sweetened Red Dye #2 to cool off to thirst quenching perfection, I would be sound asleep and having heat delirium nightmares. On the upside, there was nothing quite as invigorating as waking up to cold cherry Kool-Aide for breakfast. If the heat was truly unbearable, my mother would splurge and send me out for Carvel ice cream cones, a tricky mission when you consider the 5 block walk and the 4 flights back up to our apartment in the stifling stairwells, carrying three soft serve cones. I didn't really mind licking the melted ice cream off my arms, but sucking the drippings off my shirt left me with the lingering taste of Tide, which did not go well with rainbow sprinkles.

My mother certainly had her hands full when it came to keeping us hypothermia- and heat stroke- free in the trench-warfare environment of our apartment, but an even bigger challenge confronted her every day, and that was the care and feeding of my brother. Greg had a specific agenda, always doing things his own way, at his own pace, refusing to conform to the norms of society, even as an unborn fetus. As if in defiance of all the laws of nature and gravity, Greg had remained in utero for an extra thirty-two days, perhaps enjoying the sodium rich diet that my mother survived on for the ten month duration of her pregnancy. She claimed that licking piles of salt from her palm kept her from barfing up the saltine crackers she managed to choke down, and by the time my water-logged brother was born, he weighed in at a colossal eleven pounds and looked more like a sea sponge. I felt cheated. "Why does he look like that?" I whined. "Is there something wrong with him? Maybe the hospital gave you the wrong one! Maybe you should go back and check." I hoped that she would realize her terrible mistake, and exchange him for the good baby. I wanted a cuddly little sister that I could hold and play dress-up with, not the bloated sack of mashed potatoes that she brought home. I took an instant dislike to him and was mortified every time my mother nursed him. I would pretend to be enthralled with the evening news, or a speck on the wall. "It's ok to look", she'd say. "No, I just have something in my eye!" I'd answer defensively, squinting through my pretend temporary blindness, hands outstretched like Frankenstein.

Maybe because he gestated on a diet of pure sodium, my brother developed into toddlerhood with a warped relationship with food, and not unlike our mother, who heaved and retched her way through every waking moment of her marathon pregnancy, also had a tendency to blow chunks unexpectedly. This familial characteristic dated back as far as my Italian great grandmother Annie, who, legend has it, barfed every time she saw a man with red hair. Greg simply hated food. Given my mother's limited funds and austere culinary repertoire, there was no argument when Greg requested grilled cheese three times a day, chased down with tall glasses of Coca Cola and milk, the only meal he kept down with any regularity. My mother made no effort to expand his gastronomic horizons, for even just mentioning "baloney" or "peas and carrots" was all the prompting his delicate system needed, and she grew weary of cleaning up partially digested Wonder bread and Velveeta sandwiches. Greg was not just a picky eater, he was a slow eater. He would often spend the entire afternoon at the kitchen table, humming and daydreaming while his grilled cheese congealed and hardened, the butter soaked toast attracting flies. Every hour or so, he would take a bite and ruminate for fifteen or twenty minutes, and then restart his tuneless humming. If my exasperated mother would lose patience and ask why it was taking him so long to finish his sandwich, he would vomit, and she would have to start the whole process again.

Through diligent practice, Greg learned to puke more creatively. He would often vomit in unexpected places, like the bottom drawer of my dresser, in the deepest recesses behind my socks and secret journals, where it was sure to go unfound for weeks. "What's that damn smell?" my mother would demand every time she walked into the room. Greg would look up from his Superman comic, all dimples and gap toothed grin. "MAN!" he would exclaim, pointing to Clark Kent in the midst of ripping off his tie. Perhaps my brother envisioned himself a super hero, vanquishing enemies and big sisters alike with his mighty hurl.

As practiced as he was at ejecting stuff out, Greg just as enthusiastically worked at putting stuff in. Most days, my mother would do a thorough search of his facial orifices, checking mouth, nostrils and ears for anything suspect. Shiny objects, like nuts and bolts, keys and coins, the occasional spare refrigerator part, found their way to the moist confines of my brother's cheeks, whereas smooth, round items, such as olive pits, marbles, and even my Great Aunt Mela's cultured pearl earring nestled easily up his nose. From the mundane to the unapologetically sentimental, my brother worked feverishly to add to his collection, only to be thwarted by my mother's expert application of tweezer know-how. Once we noticed the tiny feet of a toy plastic soldier sticking out of Greg's ear, and with the skilled hand of a surgeon, my mother gently dislodged it without breaking off the wee M16 which lay precariously close to his eardrum. We were baffled by his need to sequester small objects in his face, and when my mother pressed him for an explanation, he would only say "Because they're mine."

Odd as he was, my brother was well-liked by everybody, especially grownups. After all, he was tiny and cute and he barely ate anything. He was also, for the most part, completely silent. More like a pet turtle, my brother was the perfect child. All of these attractions only made him more irritating to me. He was nearly three years old before he spoke his first words, a fact which infuriated me. My mother was unperturbed, and confident he would speak when he had something worthwhile to say, but I took it as a personal insult. I tried to encourage him in my own fashion.

"HEY! I AM YOUR SISTER, EVIE! WHAT'S WRONG WITH YOU? ARE YOU DEAF? CAN'T YOU SAY MY NAME?" I felt that screaming at him would encourage some social discourse, but he would only smile that maddeningly sweet dimpled smile at me, and later in the day, I would find his dirty socks under my pillow. One day, I returned home from school, and my mother announced that Greg had finally spoken an entire sentence.

"Wow, really? What was it?" I asked, confident they were some brotherly words of worship for me. "He said, Googem wike fish bows" my mother replied.

"GOOGEM WIKE FISH BOWS!" Greg hollered from his kitchen chair. "What's that supposed to mean?" I asked, glaring suspiciously at my greasy faced brother.

"Well, apparently he calls himself Googem, and I've been feeding him tiny pieces of smoked white fish rolled up into balls," and she demonstrated the process, popping another fish blob in his mouth. Greg screeched his delight, and patted his oily cheek. "GOOGEM!" he proclaimed again. "NO" I said, "YOU'RE GREG!" Greg ignored me and opened up for another fish ball. "Why is he calling himself that? Why can't he just say Greg like a normal person?" I demanded, imagining the implications of a brother with a speech impediment, and the effect it would have on my social life. "And why is he eating fish balls? What's wrong with grilled cheese?" I was incensed, wanting desperately to have a little brother who acted less like Greg and more like, well, me. But I was alone in my misery. Everyone thought it was adorable how he called himself Googem "It sounds like Gaugin, the great artist!" my grandmother remarked. I wondered if Gaugin had stuck rocks up his nose, or tormented his sister with smelly socks.

Greg was quite proud of his accomplishments. He had not only mastered his first sentence, he was branching out into a new world of culinary delights, and he went around announcing to anyone who would listen that he was Googem, and that he wiked fish bows. Total strangers would give my mother a bittersweet smile, as if my brother was simple or from a foreign land. The Googem phase went on for quite some time. Greg was in no hurry to branch out, savoring his new found verbosity while milking his limited dialogue for all it was worth. When he wasn't engaging complete strangers, he would sit in his Office, shuffling through his business magazines and Superman comics, pointing to the handsome and the buff, the suited and the leotarded, and proclaim "Googem wike fish bows!" reaffirming his identity with each manly man. He had found his voice, and something worth talking about, at long last.

Soon enough, Greg's vocabulary began to blossom. He was a friendly kid, and continued the tradition of introducing himself to casual passers-by.

"I'm Googem. I'm a man" he would say, usually offering a rock as a token of friendship. As he became more confident, Greg brought other characters into his monologue. He brought a toy horse to the park with us one day, and began a conversation with the mother of one of the kids playing on the swings.

"I'm Googem. This my horse" he said, as he proffered the noble plastic beast.

"Oh, how nice!" the woman answered. "What's his name?" I watched suspiciously from the nearby seesaw, knowing full well that my brother's sole purpose in life was to humiliate me.

"This my horse, Fred" he said, "Nipple Fred." The woman's eyebrows raised in bemusement as I felt myself start to black out. Greg launched into a little song and dance about his toy horse.

"They call me Fred! They call me Nipple Fred!" he sang, merrily cantering around the swing set. I clutched at my shirt, feeling as if it were my own nipples on display for the entire playground to see. The singing and cantering went on for another couple of verses, but I couldn't hear them over the sound of my own blood-curdling screams, so I was spared the horror.

As Greg matured, his vocabulary began to reflect his new interests, and he devoted himself to learning and practicing every poop word known in the English language. I redoubled my efforts to ignore him, but Greg found ingenious ways to make himself be heard.

I had spent days diligently recording my favorite songs from a transistor radio onto my new portable tape player, so I could enjoy them whenever I wanted. I waited through hours of boring commercials and DJ chatter to capture those few songs I desperately wanted to hear, and by the end of the week, I had finally recorded an hour's worth of music. At last, I retired to the bedroom, ready to sit and listen to the fruits of my labor. I pressed play, and at first, all I heard was some shuffling noises. I waited anxiously to hear the first notes of The Jackson Five's "ABC," but for a few moments, nothing happened, and then the wet sounds of my brother breathing into the microphone. Oh, no, I thought, what's this? But I already knew what to expect, and there it was, Greg's squeaky little voice, his mouth obviously pressed right up against the microphone so as not to alert anyone to his mischief.

"Sissy doody vomit sissy doody vomit sissy doody vomit. Cocky doody cocky doody cocky doody. Evie is a doody head Evie is a doody head Evie is a doody head," he whispered furtively, with unmistakable joy. I could actually hear him smiling. I slammed on the stop, then the fast forward button, and already knowing the outcome, pressed play again.

"Sissy vomit. Sissy vomit. Sissy vomit." Enraged, I brought the tape to my mother.

"Greg recorded over all my songs!" I complained. "Listen!" and I played her a portion of my brother's happy homage to excrement. Of course, her laughter only enraged me more and I decided, then and there, that it would be more satisfying to live a life of joyless, bitter resentment than to try to make another tape.

When Greg was six, he went to live with my grandparents. They said it was to help my mother out but I suspected it was because they felt sorry for me. In any case, it was a nice break from the tormenting, and I got to pretend that I was an only child for a while. For his birthday, my grandparents threw Greg a big party. My Great Aunt Teddy foolishly got Greg a chemistry set, and I looked on in horror as he opened the box with the happy children on the cover proudly beaming over a miniature volcano oozing runny red Jell-O, the Romper Room version of a deadly pyroclastic flow. Inside the box were beakers, droppers, and packets of supposedly harmless substances, but I knew, in the hands of my brother, even Jell-O could be heinous. "Oh, my! Do you think that's safe?" asked my grandmother. "Ah, c'mon, the thing is made of cardboard and pudding!" my grandfather said. "Besides, Greg's a smart kid. Right, Greg-o?" Greg beamed his most angelic smile at Ernie, and then tucked the box under his pile of birthday gifts, which included a pair of Sears Tuff-Skins Jeans and a new GI Joe with Kung Fu Grip. While the supervising adults dove into the kiddie pool-sized bowl of my grandfather's paint-peeling vodka punch, Greg slipped quietly away to his upstairs bedroom with his supposedly harmless chemical toy in tow. Later that evening, while most of the grown-ups slept off the vodka and birthday cake, my perpetually sober grandmother decided to investigate an acrid smell that was wafting from behind my brother's closed bedroom door. Once she made it past the stacks of books, magazines and old newspapers, she discovered one wall completely covered in splattered bursts of viscous, blackened gel, scorched paint hanging in sheets, the ceiling singed with snaking fingers of soot. In the middle of the floor was the plastic volcano, littered with melted plastic soldiers, chemical ooze and chunks of incinerated meat, which turned out to be the five pound rump roast my grandmother had been saving for Sunday dinner. Many years later, Greg would confess that he augmented his volcanic experiment with certain volatile household cleaners and solvents, a fact which would have driven my pacifist grandmother to beat him senseless with her favorite wooden pasta spoon. But at the time, Greg mollified her with the excuse that he was simply trying to recreate the events of AD 79 when Mount Vesuvius buried thousands of Pompeiians in one cataclysmic eruption, while paying homage to his favorite Greek demi god, Hercules. My grandmother recognized a good historical reenactment when she saw one, and putting aside the notion that you just can't make pudding explode, spared my brother the beating he deserved, and quietly brought him downstairs with her, where the two of them polished off the last of the birthday cake, careful not to disturb the slumbering party guests.

For the most part, my grandparents managed to survive Greg, and often found him a stimulating addition to the household. He engaged them in lively political conversations, discussed world events, and occasionally set fire to his comic books in the garage. Oddly enough, I missed having him around, and having no one to loathe left me with an empty feeling inside. I tried to feel the old anger and resentment, acting out by insulting my stuffed animals, calling the cats hurtful names. I even threw some of my own belongings out the window for old times' sake, but it was just no good. I couldn't muster up the energy to be truly surly, when a scant mile away, my brother was busy painting my grandparents' bathroom in red nail polish and vomiting under the couch cushions. My mother must have felt the void too, and soon had another baby. Nina was sweet and cuddly, even her spit-up was lovable, and she was everything I ever wanted in a sibling. I festooned my baby sister's head with pink ribbons, and dusted her adorable butt with baby powder, yet I remained unsatisfied. I yearned to feel vengeful, longed for the adrenaline surge of unbridled annoyance. Visits to my grandparents on the weekends would only make me feel worse, as I tried to cram in a week's worth of rage into one afternoon, desperate for any excuse to rant and complain. I know Greg did his best to accommodate my needs, but there was only so much he could accomplish in a few short hours. At the end of the day, I would go home and put a pair of my own dirty socks under my pillow.

A year later, we all ended up living with my grandparents, and at first, Greg worked enthusiastically to take up where we had left off. But all that time apart had dampened my ire, and I found myself strangely unmoved when he threw up outside my bedroom door and covered it up with newspapers. I was well into my teens now, and saving my energy for more important things, like hanging out with my friends on the stoop and perfecting our cigarette butt flicking techniques. Sensing the change in our relationship, Greg gave up trying to torment me, and we spent the remaining years of our childhood ignoring each other, ghosts of our former vindictive selves. In retrospect, it was a sad time.

Eventually, my brother and I would grow up to have a deep friendship and an abiding respect for each other, with a common love of the written word and ethnic cuisine. I often visit him and his lovely wife at their Manhattan apartment, where we share a good bottle of wine and laugh over stories of our childhood. But sometimes, despite the excellent company, I come away from these visits with a feeling of sadness and inexplicable longing. And so occasionally, before we part ways, I sneak into his bedroom and rummage through his laundry, until I find a pair of his dirty socks, which I slip into my coat pocket and carry with me for a little while. Just in case.

Googem

Gracie and Other Undesirables

It was hot, and not the lazy suburban hot that I was used to, but New York City hot, the kind of hot that reeks of melted tar, scorched cement and human suffering, the kind of hot that turns cheerful rays of sunshine into laser beams of pain reflecting off metal subway cars and burning the retinas right out of your eyes. This was New York City in the middle of August, and it was hot like I had never experienced, the kind of hot that turns gentle spirited people into murderous maniacs, and robs even the strongest of their will to live. We were sequestered in our tiny, toaster-oven apartment, my mother propped on a chair in front of the open refrigerator door, her dungarees rolled up to her knees, feet planted on the middle shelf next to a container of cottage cheese that had seen its expiration date come and go sometime around the winter solstice. She was fanning herself with the recent edition of TV guide and every once in a while would moan "Oh, God, it's hot!" I lay sprawled on the bedroom floor under the back window, hoping for a whisper of a breeze, listening to my tiny transistor radio, dripping a crime scene outline in beads of sweat. I kept my eyes closed, trying to ignore my brother, who, at the age of three, was seemingly unaffected by the grueling heat, as the very young and the feeble often are. He was stripped down to his diaper, and was making repeated trips from the bedroom to the bathroom, carrying a single grain of cat litter which he would drop in the toilet, and then send on its merry way. This was my torment:

SLAP slap slap slap slap slap slap slap slap slap... (sweaty little feet on wood)

Plunk!

Flusshhhhhhhhh...

"Yayyyyyy!"

...slap slap slap slap slap slap slap slap slap SLAP...

Rustle rustle rustle... (little fingers fishing around in the cat box)

SLAP slap slap slap slap slap slap slap slap slap...

This had been going on for the better part of the morning, and every once in a while I would muster up the energy to shout "Greg, cut it out!" but then it would take me twenty minutes to recuperate from the effort, and I was already feeling dehydrated and woozy, so I let my brother have his fun while I fantasized about ways to abandon him in the supermarket.

By noon, even Greg had grown bored with his fascinating project, and he had taken to yelling "Owwww! Owwww!" out the fire escape window to the people on the subway platform, who, deadened by the oppressive heat, pretended not to hear to hear the plaintive cries of a small child in pain. I dragged myself out of the bedroom and for a brief moment, entertained the idea of putting Greg out on the fire escape, but opted instead to nag my mother, which required significantly less energy.

"Mom, I'm bored. What can we do? Mom? What can we do? I'm bored. Mom? Mom? Mom?"

After an hour or two of this and my brother's relentless cries of mock distress, my mother stood up and shouted "That's it! If you don't shut up, we won't get a new pet."

"Hooray! A new pet! A new pet!" I shouted. "What should we get? How about a goldfish? And we can name it Goldie! And get it a pirate cave! And a plastic rock! And some blue gravel, and feed it fish food!"

"Worms! Worms! Worms!" my brother shrieked.

"How about, if you DO shut up, I won't break your legs? You wait here while I go to the pet store. Evie, take care of your brother. And don't put him on the fire escape. I will know." And my mother was out the door with her magical Pet Fund, which consisted of the week's food-shopping money and at least half a month's rent.

My mother arrived home a short time later dragging a majestic eighty pound black hairball through the door.

"Wow! What's that?" I cried, the shaggy beast lumbering over to lick my face.

"That is our new attack dog. His name is Baby. Be careful, he may not recognize you as a family member right away" my mother warned, but Baby was sprawled on his back, kicking his gigantic feet in the air, while I rubbed his tummy.

"Really? He's an attack dog? But he's so cute!"

"Guard dogs are supposed to be cute to fool the murderers. Don't you know anything?" my mother said, irritated by my lack of worldliness. Greg clambered over the dog's broad back and stuck a Matchbox car in his ear, and Baby shook his head, sending ropes of slime shooting across the floor and my brother's face. "Ewww! What's that stuff?" I cried.

"It's obviously a defense mechanism. He is trained to fend off robbers, you know" my mother said with a roll of her eyes. "Now, stop whining and go get him a bowl of water."

Baby took a few noisy laps of water and then stepped in the bowl with his giant webbed paw, emptying the contents onto my brother's bare feet. "Maybe he needs to go for a walk. Take him outside and make him pee," my mother instructed. We had no leash, but she improvised and tied a jump rope around his neck, and I headed outside with our new guard dog, eager to watch him be vicious in front of all my friends, who would, no doubt, be terrified and impressed.

Baby was in no hurry to go out into the late summer heat, choosing instead to roll around on the cool tiles in the hallway, and it took me the better part of an hour to drag him down the stairs and out of the building. By the time I got outside, all my friends had gone home for dinner, but I decided to parade him around the neighborhood just in case I met one of the bad kids from up the street. Then I could see Baby do his stuff! But Baby lay down by the curb and amused himself with a chicken bone.

"No! Bad Baby!" I yelled. "Time to make sissy!" I yanked on the rope, but Baby just lay there, panting and drooling.

"What did I say, Baby! Make sissy now!" Baby rolled in a puddle of some sticky orange liquid, ignoring my commands. I pulled with all my might to get Baby out of the gutter, and dragged him a couple of yards down the street, where he sat himself down in the shade of the building, refusing to budge. People walked by, pointing and commenting on the cute doggie, occasionally patting his giant head, which caused Baby to wag his tail and drool with even more gusto.

"Bad Baby! Very bad!" I yelled, waiting for him to remember that he was a vicious guard dog and leap into action, but he simply sat, refusing to guard, refusing to pee, drool collecting by his big hairy paws. The evening dragged on, darkness descended, and I grew weary of waiting and hauled Baby back into the building. One step inside the door, and Baby raised a leg and peed on the wall.

"No, no, no!" I cried with a stomp of my foot, and suddenly Baby was ready to head home. He dragged me tripping and stumbling up the marble stairs. Somewhere between the second and third floors, Baby dropped a dump the size of a meatloaf, and I began to suspect that he was not so well trained after all.

Our attempts to house break Baby went on for another couple of months, but for some reason, screaming at him didn't work. He refused to pee and poop outside, preferring to relieve himself in the cool, dark privacy of the stairwell. It soon became obvious to us that Baby was untrainable. In the few short months we had him, he had doubled in size and my mother could no longer keep up with his dietary demands. Oddly, a loaf of Wonder Bread a day just didn't seem to satisfy him. I watched as my mother tied the jump rope around his neck with grim resolve.

"Take him to the park and let him go," she said. I gulped back tears. Baby wasn't so bad, but spending all my valuable play time waiting for him to make doody outside had worn me down. I reluctantly took the rope and headed towards the park. Once there, I sat down on a bench by the entrance and wondered how I could just let him off the rope, left to wander and fend for his big, stupid self. I began to cry. I wrapped my arms around his neck, and buried my face in his thick, wooly coat, sobbing "I'm sorry, Baby. I'm sorry," when I was broken out of my guilt-laden reverie by the pulsing rhythm of a Salsa beat. I looked up from Baby's snot-drenched coat, and through my tears, saw a beat up old station wagon idling in the street in front of me. Inside it was a raucous family of Puerto Ricans, all of them hanging out the windows and pointing at Baby, yelling "Mira! Mira, el pero!"

The dad lowered the radio and stuck his head out the window. "Yo, mami. That's a nice dog" he said. I wiped my nose on my sleeve and rubbed the tears from my cheeks.

"You can have him," I offered with a weak smile, trying not to sound too pathetic. The children screamed with delight, and opening the door for the new addition to their already enormous family, welcomed Baby into the crowd. Baby leaped in joyfully, as if he'd found his rightful owners at last, and the father waved to me and drove away. I stood there for a few minutes, staring in disbelief as they drove off down Bronx Park East, Salsa music fading into the distance, the overloaded, sagging car finally carrying Baby out of sight. I walked down Allerton Avenue, half expecting to see the car around every corner with the door open, Baby getting shoved to the curb. But they were gone, and I sprinted the rest of the way home, eager to tell my amazing story.

"Yeah, right" my mother said, "Where's the dog?"

"With the Puerto Ricans!" I reiterated.

"Bullshit" my mother said. "Everybody knows Puerto Ricans hate dogs."

"No, these Puerto Ricans like dogs! Really!"

My mother refused to believe that my story could possibly be true, and accused me of not only making it all up, but also that I must have profited from the transaction, which involved a mysterious wealthy benefactor and not the carload of dead beats I obviously fabricated.

"What do you think, I'm stupid? That was one valuable dog! You don't just give a dog like that away!" she said as she emptied my pockets, only to find only a piece of Bazooka gum and three cents.

"But you told me to give him away!" I argued.

"Yes, but not to Puerto Ricans! Jesus Christ, do I have to do everything myself?" My mother chalked the whole thing up to ineptitude and naiveté, and vowed to recoup her losses from any birthday, Christmas and graduation money I might receive in the future.

It wasn't long after the Baby experience that my mother started craving a new and exotic pet, and she announced to me and Greg that we would be getting a monkey. How cool! I thought. I will be the envy of all my friends, walking around with a monkey on my shoulder. Maybe we could even teach him to dance and collect coins in a cup! My mother's boyfriend, Batman, began constructing the monkey's enclosure in our living room, a ceiling-high cage with multi-level platforms and a door big enough for a man to fit through. It took up half the room, and soon, our refrigerator was filled with strange smelling fruits and containers of writhing worms. Batman drove my mother to the pet store, and they arrived home with a squirrel monkey enclosed in a cardboard box with holes. Greg and I crowded around the box, where we could see the soft brown eyes peering out, inquisitive and intelligent.

"Now, listen, let's give him some room. He may be nervous at first," my mother said. I asked what we should name him, and my mother, carefully opening the box, said his name was Dondi. "Hi, Dondi," I said, softly to the box, hoping the endearing little fella would bond instantly with me. And in the next moment, a screaming blur of monkey fur came tearing out of the carrier, and Dondi was up the curtains in a flash. We stood back in shock as the monkey, perching himself up by the ceiling, shrieked and peed all over the curtains. Instinctively, I knew this was going to be bad.

The pet shop owner assured us that Dondi needed to go through a period of readjustment, but I was convinced that this monkey was not a people lover. Dondi sat for days, balled up in a high corner of his cage, arms wrapped around his head, rocking, rocking, rocking, waiting for someone to get too close. We would be greeted by his enraged screaming as he rushed the bars of his cage, followed by a well aimed stream of monkey pee. Feeding time was even less enjoyable. Dondi would squish the banana chunks in his angry little fist and fling them at the wall. Meal worms would go rocketing through the air and pelt us as we fled the room.

My mother thought perhaps Dondi was frustrated by his confinement, and he just needed to get a little exercise, so, one afternoon, she foolishly opened his cage door and let him out. For a few hours, it was like a free for all in the psycho ward, as Dondi once again perched atop the curtain rod, and screaming victoriously, flung his poo at us and shredded the curtains with his nasty little teeth. We hid in the bathroom until Batman came over to help us recapture the crazed little monkey, who, by then, had destroyed the couch cushions and peed on the television. Batman threw a blanket over him, and flung him back into his cage, only to be rewarded with a chunk of papaya to the neck.

And so it was that Dondi went to live on the "Farm," a mysterious place in an undisclosed "upstate" location that welcomed animal rejects with open arms, no matter how untrained or destructive, antisocial or vicious. Dondi's cage was taken down, poo cleaned off the walls and our cats, at long last, came out from hiding under the bed.

After that, my mother stuck to pets that were less likely to assault us with fecal matter. We'd been through a string of other pets in an attempt to find a "friend" for our stalwart Siamese cat, Py, but we were yet to find a good match. Py outlasted them all, including Om, the freakishly friendly seal-point that enjoyed being mauled by our mongrel terrier Ralph. Om would deliberately flaunt her uplifted butt in Ralph's face, and Ralph would happily oblige by chewing on her heisted heiny, a disturbing spectacle for even the most seasoned animal lover. My mother just couldn't tolerate a masochistic cat, so she sent Om to live with a friend of mine who gave her the more respectable name of Juliette. The name change didn't alter Om's deviant tendencies, though, and my friends' family was horrified when they found the cat sitting on the kitchen table in a bowl of steaming hot chicken soup. And with no willing cat to chew on, poor Ralph became despondent and started gnawing holes in the apartment floor. My mother grew tired of pulling splinters out of Ralph's tongue, and soon sent him to live on the "Farm" as well. I was sad to see Ralph go, but my mother assured me he would have a great life there, running in the fields, making friends with all the other depraved dogs.

My mother quickly filled the void with a new pet. Gracie the cat came into our lives with all the charm and personality of a fur-covered block of cheese. At first, we were baffled by her cold, standoffish behavior. We believed, with patience, love and fish balls we would win her affection, but Gracie completely shunned human contact, and would recoil at the first sign of an approaching stroke. Scratches under the chin, vigorous ear rubbing, even a warm, inviting lap were all met with the same dull, apathetic expression. Gracie would not play with the catnip mouse, or the ever popular feather on a fishing pole, would not even chase the big, slow cockroaches that paraded across the floor right in front of her nose. Gracie gave no indication that she was actually a cat. She never meowed, never purred, never even hissed or spit. She just sat, emotionless and unresponsive, like a cat-shaped hand bag. With no justifiable excuse to get rid of her, my mother had to let Gracie stay on indefinitely.

Gracie lived under our roof for years, unmoved and unmoving, never changing, always greeting us with the same blank expression of unrecognizing mistrust. We speculated that she must have some kind of brain damage, how else could she resist our charms? We gave up trying to convince her we were good people, that we were worthy of her attention. We accepted her scorn, and resigned ourselves to her silent, unequivocal rejection, until one fateful day, years after she first dropped into our lives like a well aimed brick, Gracie quite unexpectedly came to life.

It was a warm Sunday morning when we awoke to a horrific noise. Leaping out of bed, my mother raced to the kitchen to investigate, and found Gracie rolling around on the linoleum like a kitten, paws kneading the air, a look of pure joy replacing her normally stony expression. I came up behind my mother, afraid of what I might find, only to witness Gracie's bizarre transformation. "What's wrong with Gracie? And what made that terrible sound?" I asked my mother, as we cautiously peered around the kitchen door. My mother took a tentative step towards the writhing cat. "Gracie?" she said, reaching out to touch her, when the cat righted herself, looked into my mother's eyes and let loose a sound that made us jump back in horror, a full-throated manly bellow with an undertone of sheer agony. "Holy crap, what was that?" my mother shouted, holding a protective arm in front of me, as if the cat might suddenly detonate. Gracie made the sound again, this time raising her rump high into the air, pedaling her back feet, a pathetic imploring look on her face. "Oh, for chrissake, the goddamn cat's in heat", my mother said. "What does that mean?" I shouted over the cat's deafening screams. "It means she wants to make babies. She'll get over it in a few days", my mother yelled, hands clapped over her ears.

But days turned into weeks, and Gracie continued to announce her readiness to procreate with all the gusto of someone being burned at the stake. We learned to readjust our speaking volume, shouting entire conversations until our throats were raw.

"WOULD YOU PASS THE SALT?" (MAAAHHH! MAAAHHH! MAAAHHH!)

"WHAT?" (MAAAHHH! MAAAHHH! MAAAHHH!)

"I SAID, WOULD YOU PASS THE SALT?" (MAAAHHH! MAAAHHH! MAAAHHH!)

We quickly grew weary of trying to be heard over Gracie's constant and unrelenting tirade, and found it was just easier to get up and get the salt, and skip the conversation.

After a month, when we all began to suffer from hearing loss, my mother caved and took Gracie to the vet. Gracie continued her rhythmic screams from inside the cardboard carrier, and people in the waiting room glared at my mother as if she were somehow responsible for the disturbing din. "Can't you make that stop?" one irate woman asked, her little Chihuahua shivering miserably. "Yeah, right. That's why I'm wasting my time sitting here with you," my mother barked back.

It was Gracie's turn, and my mother brought her into the examination room, where the flinching doctor extracted her from the box.

"WHAT SEEMS TO BE THE PROBLEM?" he bellowed over the screaming.

"ARE YOU KIDDING?" my mother asked.

"WELL, IT APPEARS SHE IS IN HEAT" the vet stated redundantly.

"NO SHIT. HOW LONG WILL IT LAST?"

The good doctor could not provide my mother with a definitive answer. Apparently, her endocrine system had been stuck in the off position, and now that it was switched on, it was making up for lost time with a vengeance. Gracie's condition was an enigma, and how long her misery would continue was anybody's guess.

In fact, Gracie the cat screamed through the entire summer and into the fall, at which point, she suddenly reverted to her vegetative state, as if nothing had happened. The relief was immense. We slept soundly, enjoying quiet nights of peaceful dreams, spoke in hushed tones, listened to classical music softly playing on the radio. We deluded ourselves into thinking the change was permanent, and that in one massive hormonal surge, Gracie had purged herself of wanton lust. We reveled in her silence, and prayed she would stay that way forever.

It would be years before Gracie's gonads kicked into high gear again, and by that time we had all moved in with my grandparents. My mother's basement apartment had a lovely view of Ernie's garden, and Py spent her days stretched out on the window sill, enjoying the sunshine and the smell of greenery. There was no visible change in Gracie's demeanor, and although she sat in front of the screen door staring into the yard, she remained unresponsive to the chirping of birds and the occasional visiting squirrel. Life was peaceful.

And then the inevitable happened. I could hear the screaming from my third floor bedroom, followed by my mother's muffled "son of a bitch!" as Gracie's tiny, twisted pituitary gland announced it was time to make a go of reproduction once again. And this time, it meant business.

By the second week of Gracie's quest for fertilization, every Tom cat within a three mile radius was taking up residence in Ernie's back yard, making their presence known to anyone with a nose. The big boys were stalking and strutting, and spraying their testosterone drenched urine all over the brick wall underneath my mother's garden window. Gracie screamed and screamed, the boys sprayed and sprayed, and my mother resorted to closing her one and only window against the noxious fumes. She tried blasting the Toms with a water gun, but there was nothing that would keep them away for very long, not with this ripe female only inches away from conquest. My mother watched the horny cats stake out her back door, just waiting for an opportunity to show Gracie who her daddy was. And then, one night, Gracie the cat decided she could no longer resist their charms.

The morning dawned, sunny and peaceful, the song of chickadees and mourning doves filled the air. My mother awoke, immediately sensing that something was not quite right. She looked around, located Py sitting in a patch of sunlight on the floor, but something was amiss. Why was it so...quiet? She got up to investigate, and discovered the screen in the back door had been ripped to shreds. My mother stuck her head through the tattered screen and called out tentatively, "Gracie?" But she was gone. Gracie had literally torn her way out, and run off with her pack of eager suitors during the night. My mother thought she ought to search the neighborhood, but reconsidered, realizing how much she was enjoying the peace, the absence of agonizing howls. She sat on her bed and lit a cigarette, then opened her garden window to let in the morning breeze, which smelled refreshingly free of cat urine.

That evening, my mother patched up the screen with some duct tape and even closed the inside door, worried that Gracie might suddenly make a comeback and try to shred her way back into our lives. But Gracie never returned and we all breathed a collective sigh of relief. My mother spent the next few days extolling the virtues of the single pet household, claiming she was done with strange and exotic animals forever. But before the week was up, she acquired Willy, a sickly ferret with explosive diarrhea. My mother found him irresistible. "Don't worry, you'll get used to the smell!" she assured me, clutching a towel to her face and judiciously spraying the room with Glade Pine Forest Air Freshener. By the third day, Willy had gone off to live on the Farm with Ralph the perverted the dog and Dondi the psychotic monkey where, for all I know, they are still cavorting in the fields and making friends with all the other undesirables.

A Night Out with the Chickens

I was looking good in my kelly-green maxi dress and my peace-sign choker, standing outside our building with my brother, who was as dressed up as he could manage in elastic-waisted jeans and a Superman pajama top. I was hoping some of my friends would notice me standing there and wonder to what exotic destination I might be bound, for it was obvious that I was waiting for my ride and that we were going someplace really great. I kept checking my reflection in passing car windows, flipping my still damp hair off my shoulder to emphasize the fact that I had even showered for the occasion. Some of the filthier boys rode by on their bikes and stared at me like they'd never seen a person dressed to attend a fancy affair before, but then my grandmother pulled up, and my brother and I piled in to the front seat without a single one of my girlfriends catching a glimpse of my new outfit. I stuck my head out the window in a last ditch effort to be noticed going out so late on a school night, but everyone was home having dinner. Yes, all my less-fortunate friends were home, sitting down to hum drum meals like Shake 'n Bake and Hamburger Helper, while I, dressed up and smelling of Jean Nate, was going out to dinner at the ever-fashionable Hampton House in glamorous Parkchester, where career gals lived and worked and shopped at expensive stores like Macy's. I felt grown up and attractive, and I eagerly looked forward to an evening out with my grandmother and her sisters. There would be Shirley Temples and good conversation, which, to a nine year old, meant lots of face squeezing and staining of cheeks with rainbow lipstick smears, and best of all, substantial cash rewards.

My aunts would arrive at the restaurant before us, having reserved their favorite table in the very front by the window, where they could be seen enjoying cocktails and breadsticks by all the hardworking folks on their way home from work. They would jockey for the best positions, always leaving the uncomfortable, thigh-sticking vinyl bench for me and my brother, but we liked being tucked behind this way, where no one could see us slipping Sweet 'n Lows and butter pats into our pockets. As soon as we settled in to our seats, my Great Aunt Olga would quickly maneuver to establish herself in the dominant Aunt position.

"Are you being a good girl in school? Yeah? Good for you! Here, here, don't tell anybody....," and she would press a dollar bill into my palm under the table, her hand all warm and bony, and strangely powerful for her diminutive size.

"You keep that for yourself!" she would announce in her best stage whisper, and make a show of firmly patting my closed fist. This was, of course, to show her sisters that she was the one who loved me best, and worthy of the most devotion in return. Then she would motion my brother over from across the table.

"Greg. Greg." Waving her hand, her perfect polished fingernails looking strangely out of place against all those veins and wrinkles, she would jerk her head in a conspiratorial way.

"Come here, my favorite nephew," she would croon, and Greg would dutifully climb down from the red vinyl bench, crawl under the table and pop up, all dimples and smiles, and accept the two quarters she pushed into his little fist. Aunt Olga would then grab a handful of his face, plant her crimson lipstick mark, and whisper in his ear "Don't forget who your favorite auntie is!"

This process would continue until each one of our great aunts had asked us the obligatory questions and then slipped us the bribe that would keep them in the alpha position. It was a ritual we knew and loved, hamming it up and acting surprised every time.

"Wow, Aunt Teddy! Thank you! I'm saving up for a new transistor radio!"

"Gee, Aunt Mela, thank you so much! I'm going to put it in my piggy bank!"

But once the hand outs were done, Greg and I would slip away to the counter side of the restaurant where we would purchase candy from the glass display case and stuff our pockets full. Sometimes we would head downstairs to the bathroom and eat as much of it as we could before dinner. By the time we sat back down at the table, Aunt Olga would be on her second martini, and instigating fights that would carry on throughout the evening. With only a slight variation in theme, they had practically the same argument every week, and seemingly unaware that they were in a public place, my aunts would hollar at each other at the top of their lungs.

"Vera, I did what you said, and I caught a mouse in the mouse trap. And I can tell you this, you were wrong. I know for a fact that mouse had bones!" Aunt Olga waved her finger in Googie's direction.

"Olga, I never told you mice had no bones," my grandmother countered with indignation.

"Yes! Yes you did! I remember it clearly. You said, 'Olga, mice have no bones, and that's why they can crawl up through the walls and get into your apartment. Because they have no bones.' I remember!"

"I would never say that! And why would you believe anything so stupid?" my grandmother flung back, bringing the argument to the next level.

"Oh, so you're saying I'm stupid? You think I'm stupid?"

And this would be the general tone of the evening. My brother and I would eat all the breadsticks and wash them down with our constantly replenished Shirley Temples, quietly excusing ourselves to visit the bathroom and eat more candy as the Principe sisters engaged in heated debate.

Although there were only four of them at the table, my grandmother grew up in a family of seven girls. Two baby brothers never made it past infancy, and their father died in his mid-thirties of a strange and rare genetic disease that he unknowingly passed on to four of his daughters, which rendered his girls physically underdeveloped, sterile, and prone to growing lumps where they shouldn't be. The eldest, my Great Aunt Mela, was all of four foot five, and the first to be afflicted. By the time she had graduated college, and began a career teaching Spanish to high schoolers, it was obvious that she was destined to look like a fifth grader for the rest of her life. Not long after, an operation to remove a growth from her throat left her mouth scarred and twisted, and her voice sounding like she'd been gargling rocks. The effect was disconcerting, given her tiny stature and her school marmish demeanor. I felt bad for Aunt Mela, but when she called me over to shower me with Spanish endearments, I flinched, just the same.

"OH, MI CORAZON! MI AMOR! MI TESORO!" she croaked affectionately, her ruined vocal chords banging against each other, the sound of a train wreck made flesh. Pressing her lumpy, purple lip against my cheek, I obediently accepted her kisses, wondering how something so little could produce such a cacophony. But despite her size, it was obvious that Aunt Mela was the matriarch of the bunch, and never, ever to be trifled with.

The Chickens

"VERA, YOU OWE ME THIRTY SEVEN CENTS FROM LAST WEEK."

"Mela, why don't we just figure it out when the bill comes?"

"NO, LET'S DO IT NOW. ALSO, I HAVE A COUPON FOR YOU. IT'S TEN CENTS OFF FLEISHMAN'S MARGARINE. SO THAT MAKES FORTY SEVEN CENTS YOU OWE ME."

My grandmother would dutifully count out the change, realizing the futility of arguing with Mela, who, being the oldest in a family of seven females, was used to making demands and getting her way.

"Mela, I don't have enough change."

"OH, JUST GIVE ME A DOLLAR, AND I'LL PAY YOU THE DIFFERENCE NEXT TIME. TEDDY, YOU SHORTED THE TIP LAST WEEK BY SEVENTEEN CENTS. PUT OUT AN EXTRA QUARTER TONIGHT, AND OLGA CAN GIVE YOU THE EIGHT CENTS BACK FROM THE MONEY SHE OWES YOU FOR THE DIME YOU LENT VERA FOR THE METER TWO WEEKS AGO."

"Mela, what are you talking about? I don't owe Teddy anything! I bought those support hose for her last month, and she still hasn't paid me back."

Fighting over money generally went on for the better part of the evening, the debates fueled by decades of power struggles and long-held grudges. It was a complex process, kept organized by a detailed list of checks and balances written in Aunt Mela's scrawling penmanship. Always a spinster, she seemed to be passionate about only one thing: ruling her sisters with an iron fist.

Next in line was Aunt Teddy, who favored very loud pantsuits and chain smoked through the entire dinner. The effect of all those psychedelic colors and swirling clouds of smoke was quite mesmerizing, and no matter where she went, Aunt Teddy seemed to bring her own festive carnival atmosphere. Unlike her elder, malformed sister, Aunt Teddy was a blonde bombshell, at least she was back in the twenties when she was a "flapper" and wore scandalously short dresses and too much lipstick. She also had a handsome husband who died many years earlier, in a way no one in my family would discuss in front of me. Aunt Teddy believed the ghost of her dead husband was in her bedroom closet, and she would hold séances there to try and contact him. I thought it was all very sad and romantic, until I learned that my great uncle had, in fact, died in that very bedroom, right on top of her. I looked at Aunt Teddy with different eyes after that, not quite sure how to feel about my sweet elderly aunt who had killed her husband with sex.

Next in line was Aunt Olga, who was the typical middle child, always wanting to be the center of attention, never feeling loved enough. As the second daughter to carry the mysterious disease, she, too, was without womanly attributes. Family folk lore had it that Aunt Olga was engaged to a cute guy back when she was young and attractive, but her incessant neediness drove him off before he even found out that she had neither breasts nor functioning ovaries, and that was the end of her romantic affairs. Aunt Olga fairly demanded to be loved, and whenever possible, waited on hand and foot. At the restaurant, she would wave her martini glass over her head, a stony expression on her face, until it was fetched away by the never attentive-enough waiter, whose tip would suffer in the absence of his undivided devotion to her needs. Aunt Olga had a giant tumor on her liver, giving her the belly of a woman six months pregnant, but she managed to live with it for quite a long time. I was convinced that she chose her stylish belted outfits specifically to accentuate her swollen abdomen, perhaps enjoying the attention it drew from strangers unaccustomed to seeing a woman in her sixties ripe with child.

As if the bulging belly wasn't odd enough, Aunt Olga also lacked a functioning stomach. Doctors removed it when it too became diseased, another target of the family legacy. When Aunt Olga ate, food dropped out of her esophagus like cluster bombs from a B52, landing unfettered and ungoverned into a "pseudo stomach." This caused her to belch uncontrollably, an experience she called "dumping," and copious amounts of digestive juices would go rocketing back up into her mouth. When she pressed two fingers to her throat and screwed up her face from the bitter regurgitation, we all knew this was the universal sign for "bile." I tried diligently to ignore the sights and sounds of my great aunt working her way through her plate of veal scallopini, but she invariably felt the need to share the state of her digestive processes. "I'm having bile!" she would announce to all within earshot. Aunt Olga took the discomfort out of her dining experience by getting hammered, but gin did not make her personality any easier for the rest of the world to swallow.

Noticeably absent from the table were the two sisters who preceded my grandmother, one of whom, Aunt Winney, had recently died from complications of a surgical procedure to remove some of those omnipresent lumps. My unfortunate aunt had gone in for a fairly routine surgery, only to go home with the unwanted gift of hospital issue sponges left inside her body cavity. The next youngest sister, Aunt Dorothy, had broken with tradition and moved away to the Pacific Northwest where she married a farmer. Although Aunt Dorothy had a long and amicable marriage, and bore several happy, healthy children, her decision to move to rural Oregon was a source of endless derision from her city dwelling sisters.

"Did I tell you I got a letter from Dorothy? Evidently one of their cows died last week."

"Cows? What does Dorothy know about cows? What does she think, she's better than us? It's no wonder that cow died. Do you remember how afraid she was of that cat Aunt Ida had? Dorothy always hated animals."

"Aunt Ida never had a cat, it was a poodle."

"She never had a poodle! It was a cat, and Dorothy was terrified of it."

"Olga, what does Aunt Ida's cat have to do with Dorothy?"

"Vera, will you stop interrupting? I was trying to make a point!"

The sisters would pontificate on Dorothy and her bumpkin husband and their unsophisticated kids, discussing the inevitable maiming and disfiguring they would suffer due to too much time spent outdoors. Whispered asides about "animal husbandry" were enough to make my blood run cold. To me, they were the most terrifying family in the world. How could it be I was related to people who killed their own chickens? Recent pictures of them passed around at dinner revealed a blonde, freckle-faced bunch, all clad in flannel shirts and cowboy hats. They might as well have been Moon people, they were that foreign.

The youngest sister in the clan was Florrie, my grandmother's favorite, and the one who received the heaviest dose of rotten genes. The ticking time bomb that lived in her DNA quite suddenly exploded when she was still in her twenties, causing her lovely brown eyes to bulge, her slender nose to swell, and her petite figure to expand to elephantine proportions, confounding her doctors. Without a diagnosis, poor Aunt Florrie just got bigger and stranger looking, until she was hospitalized and hooked up to multiple tubes and machines in an effort to make her body stop it's bizarre rampage of growth. Bedridden and failing, Florrie was visited by her husband, Bill, who, disgusted by his once-lovely young wife's suddenly ballooning appearance, called her a "fat cow," causing Florrie to strike out in anger and fall out of bed. This was said to set off a series of catastrophic events on her already ravaged body, and Florrie never went home from the hospital. Needless to say, Bill's name became anathema in the Principe family, invoking the "corno," the devil's horn, and the evil eye every time it was mentioned, and they would just as soon have run him through with a meat fork as set eyes on him again. But Bill managed to catch himself another cutie who was a longtime family friend, and they were forced to endure his presence at holiday gatherings, and in deference to their friend, exchange pleasantries. This caused the Principe girls no end of grief, as every time they looked at his smarmy face, they were reminded of their darling sister and her tragic demise.

At this point in the tale, anybody with a shred of decency in their soul shouts out, "My God, what a tragedy!" but it is also at this point that the story takes a decidedly Italian turn, for in an ironic twist of fate, Bill, who was so offended by the sight of his grotesque dying wife, slowly began to go blind, and so it was because of his failing vision that he accidentally stepped off the train platform and right into the path of an oncoming Lexington Avenue Express. The six Principe sisters attended his funeral, and sat in the front pew by his coffin like a stone wall of pure Italian vengeance, all silent, and all smiling.

"Oh, yes, we smiled. We smiled like it was the happiest day of our lives," my grandmother would recall, her eyes shining with vindication, a look I never saw except when she told the story of Bill and the number 5 train. As horrifying as it was, I enjoyed this tale of divine retribution, and felt proud to call it a dark chapter in my family history.

And so, every Wednesday, the remaining sisters had their hair and nails done, and gathered together to dine and complain and holler at each other and fight over money, and at the end of the evening, my grandmother would chauffer her sisters to their respective apartments. They would pile in the back of the car, all skinny legs and beauty parlor coiffs, bickering and clucking, shuffling brown bags of leftovers. Aunt Mela would be the first to get dropped off, and I would escort her up to the building, where she would give me another lumpy misshapen kiss on the cheek. I sometimes wondered why Aunt Mela had never found herself a nice little Italian guy, why there was never any family whisperings of love gone awry, or even a hint of an idescretion for the oldest sister. Many years later, going through a box of dusty faded photos, I would find some racy shots of her at an upstate camp for young ladies, wearing a fairly revealing bathing costume, long hair cascading down over her shoulders. Her back was arched, cheesecake style, and she was giving the camera a shockingly seductive look. I remember laughing out loud, thinking, "Why, Aunt Mela, you vamp!" and then wondering, who could it have been taking the photo? Turning it over, I discovered an inscription. "My Darling, you are so lovely! I love you forever, Beatrice." My initial reaction was surprise and disbelief, but the more I thought about it, the sadder it seemed. Aunt Mela had found herself someone who cared not one bit about her broken reproductive system, who no doubt found her no nonsense, take charge approach to life quite endearing. In more enlightened times, Aunt Mela might have had herself a wife. Instead, she kept her passion hidden, and died in the apartment she had lived alone in for over forty years, taking her secret with her, and leaving a brand new orthopedic bed and her Chinese figurines to her cleaning lady.

Aunt Olga would get dropped off next, and thanks to the three or four martinis, would require door to door service. She would lean heavily on my arm all the way up on the elevator to her 5th floor apartment, where she would conspire to get me to come inside for a few minutes while she carefully hung her coat and eased herself down onto the couch. She would pop off her perfectly accessorized belt, freeing the incongruous belly bulge to slide into a more comfortable position, and let out a sigh of relief. Several years later, that bulge would be her undoing, and according to her wishes, there would be a grandiose Catholic funeral with priests waving censers and pipe organs playing mournful Ave Marias. Aunt Teddy, having found her way to the service at St. Raymond's despite advanced dementia, waited for the pall bearers to carry her sister's body down the aisle, and during a moment of hushed silence, stood up and yelled across the church, "Hey, Vera! I'm hungry! Ya got a boloney sandwich?" My beleaguered grandmother managed to dig up a cough drop from her purse, and so keep her confused sister preoccupied until the service was over.

Aunt Teddy was always eager to get home from the weekly dinner, supposedly to watch her beloved Mets on TV, but I suspected she really just wanted to hang around the bedroom closet and shoot the breeze with her sorely-missed dead husband. My grandmother would wait until we saw her wave cheerfully to us from her apartment window, a stream of cigarette smoke curling up from her outstretched hand. A bum colon would ultimately send her to her great reward, and for her funeral, she had requested that her coffin be closed and adorned with photos from her happy past. My favorite was one of her standing outside on a summer day holding her baby boy, smiling broadly and squinting into the camera, her blonde hair catching the sun. "Leave it to Teddy," I heard my grandmother complain to a friend. "Always so vain, she couldn't even have an open casket!" The thought of Aunt Teddy's waxen, stiff corpse on view for all to see filled me with horror, and I grabbed a gilt-framed image of her in a short, flashy flapper dress from the top of the coffin. I clung to it throughout the day, sneaking peeks at her daringly exposed knees to ward off the mental image of mortuary tables and drainage tubes. I was grateful for Aunt Teddy's vanity, and hoped her spirit was at peace in a happy place, maybe having a nooner with her beloved husband back in the bedroom closet.

My brother and I were the last to be driven home, and we would arrive at the building full and sleepy, our pockets bulging with candy and cash and sugar packets. Googie would lean over and drop a couple more lipstick bombs on the battlefields of our cheeks, and send us off bearing packages of leftovers up to our apartment, where my mother would shake us down for the money she knew we had gotten that evening.

"Fork it over" she would say as soon as we were inside the door.

"What?" I would pretend to have no idea what she was talking about, attempting to dodge the interrogation by heading straight for the bedroom.

"Get over here and gimme the cash!" my mother would demand, and I would reluctantly empty my pockets down to the last penny.

"Here," she would say, handing me back a couple of quarters. "Go buy me a pack of cigarettes. But first wipe that lipstick off your face. It looks like you were in a fight to the death with Aunt Mela's lip."

One particular time I went to the store in my fancy dress and my velvet choker, with Passionate Plum and Candy Apple Red smeared across my cheeks, my gaudy badges of love on display for all to see, fighting back tears of frustration. By the time I reached Mr. Rosenblum's candy store, my eyes were swollen and red, my nose was bright pink, and the lipstick stains were streaked with snot. Mr. Rosenblum looked at me with mild disgust, and handing me a pack of Marlboros and a nickel change, said "Who beat you up?"

"My mother" I blurted out, and it was worth the terrible pang of guilt to see the look of surprise on Mr. Rosenblum's face.

The Chickens

The Cooking Lesson

I stood nervously at the stove, clutching a wooden-handled spatula in one hand and a can of solid Crisco shortening in the other, beads of sweat forming along my hairline in worried anticipation. Behind me, my mother stood breathing down my neck, ready to pounce if I didn't follow her explicit directions. The dented aluminum frying pan was smoking hot, ready for the next step, but I hesitated.

"Go ahead" my mother urged. "And don't be stingy with the Crisco!"

I cautiously dropped a spoonful of fat onto the scalding hot surface, and my mother grabbed the spatula out of my hand.

"What, are you paying for it?" she yelled, and scooping a grapefruit sized portion out of the can, slapped it confidently into the pan, where it melted on contact.

"Now, quick! Hand me the matzoh," she commanded, and I passed her the chipped ceramic bowl containing the gooey cracker and egg mixture. She expertly slid the wet mess into the lake of grease, turned the flame down to the size of a match head, and grabbing me by the arm, walked us out of the kitchen. "The secret is you gotta forget the stuff is cooking on the stove. Don't even look at it! Otherwise, it's just no good." I obediently stood back, filled with awe and anxiety, as she bundled my brother into his stroller, and before taking him out for a nice leisurely walk, waved a cautionary finger at me. "If you touch it, I'll know." And she left me there, hovering in the kitchen doorway, trying to ignore the sizzling pan on the stove and biting my fingernails. I knew my first obligation was to follow my mother's all important instructions, so I decided to distract myself by watching cartoons. I settled myself on the floor in front of the TV and tried to put the matzoh out of my mind by focusing instead on Magilla Gorilla. But it was impossible. How could I concentrate on a pet shop ape in a fedora when there was an all consuming drama unfolding in the kitchen? I just couldn't stop myself. I was drawn back to the stove, held captive by the song of this golden, greasy siren, and, placing my face inches from the pan, breathed deep the heady aroma. I desperately wanted to stick the spatula in and peek at the newly formed crust on the bottom, to hear the hiss as the still sticky wet layer met the blazing hot surface, volcanic fat bubbling up the sides of the pan. The stress was grueling, but I forced myself to sit back down, and wait patiently at the table, listening to the musical sizzle and pop, oblivious to the blaring TV and little Ogee's never ending pleas to purchase the ridiculous ape, and so release him once and for all from his tiny store front prison.

I had plenty of time for reflection while I waited for my mother's return. She never rushed the cooking process, and in the case of the masterpiece spattering hot fat in front of me, her patience produced something so extraordinary that I begged to be shown its mysterious secrets.

My mother's matzoh brei was her one shining moment of culinary glory, the singular event that brought her comatose cooking muse back from the brink of death. Bold in her extravagant use of hydrogenated fats, my mother also had the extraordinary ability to walk away, leaving her creation alone and unmolested. On school days, when

The Cooking Lesson

I arrived home starving, out of breath and salivating with anticipation, my mother would dish out a steaming plate for me, then dowse it with a handful of kosher salt, and running the risk of a blistered palate, I would shovel the crispy, steaming ambrosia down, hoping to have a second helping before having to sprint back to school. Some days, I made a game effort for thirds, but my mother usually ushered me hastily out the door, yelling "Hurry up, you're gonna be late! Don't run, you'll get cramps! Button your coat!" And I would fly down the stairs, savoring the salty grease that lingered on my lips.

Back in school, I would sit behind my antiquated ink well desk, bloated, panting, and just a little nauseous from the mad dash. I would look around with pity at all my classmates who had suffered through mediocre lunches of left over tuna surprise and soggy baloney sandwiches while I enjoyed another slippery onion flavored burp. But in the back of my mind, I always knew this contentment was short lived.

For the magical cooking muse that possessed my mother when she took out that box of Streit's Onion Matzoh promptly slipped back into her deep coma afterwards, depleted from the effort, her creative muse juices all dried up. It was for good reason that our utensil drawer contained no peeler, no paring knife, no well worn butcher block cutting board, as my mother believed fresh fruits and vegetables were enemies of her valuable creative energy, and as outdated as nylon stockings. Her cooking tool of choice was a third generation can opener, the gears deeply encrusted with years of fossilized tomato sauce and cat food. It had a bottle opener on the bottom end that would carve a V-shaped gouge into her palm every time she jammed its worn out blade into the lip of a can, but my mother refused to give it up in favor of, say, a bag of crispy carrots or nice head of lettuce. My mother's love of canned vegetables brought many an uninspired meal to the table, and it was often with disappointment and resignation that I climbed the stairs for lunch, waiting for the welcoming song of spatula against fry pan and the hypnotizing scent of fried onion, only to find a steaming pot of lifeless canned spinach, boiled to the point of being unrecognizable as anything that actually grew out of the good earth and reduced to a mass of bubbling dark matter, then mixed in with a generous sprinkling of Hungry Jack Potato Buds, turning it the color and consistency of pond scum. The mere sight of this heinous concoction brought tears to my eyes, but my mother insisted it was a valuable source of vitamins and minerals, touting the virtues of the noble leafy green and the humble spud, two vegetables that could only have less in common with this dish if they had been passed through an atom smasher and then shot onto the surface of the sun. Often, my brother would vomit his first bite right back into the bowl, with no visually discernable difference between the yet-to-be eaten and the partially digested. I would attempt to shoot the stuff right past my tongue and down my throat, willing to risk death by asphyxiation rather than let it come in direct contact with my taste buds. Despite our relentless protests, my mother served "Spinach Mash" to us on a regular basis, insisting it was an acquired taste, one that we would grow up to love and appreciate once our palates had matured. But I noticed she never actually ate the stuff herself.

Back at the kitchen table, vivid thoughts of Spinach Mash caused my head to hurt and my growling stomach to lurch. I put my head down on the table and, listening to the soothing hiss of hot fat, I let my thoughts wander. I thought about my desk mate at school, Peter Everhardt, who almost always had his pinky finger jammed in his nostril up to the second knuckle. I would watch Peter out of the corner of my eye, wondering what he would do with the prize once he found it. But dwelling on Peter's disgusting extractions didn't help my frame of mind. The warm sun pouring in the kitchen window was making me sleepy, and I began to doze, daydreaming of the frozen food section at the A & P, where, on Friday nights, my mother would let us pick out whatever we wanted from the exciting selection of Swanson TV Dinners. It was a tough choice, but I usually went for the Salisbury steak, which sounded fancy, like something vacationers might eat at a Swiss ski resort. I loved how the individual compartments kept the courses separated, my rectangle of chopped beef swimming in its own island of beige gravy, while off to the left, a neat section of mashed potatoes remained isolated and unsullied. I enjoyed the complete control I had over my dinner, and as dictator of my little aluminum kingdom, I decreed that mingling of food was strictly forbidden.

The best part of the self contained three course dinner was the tiny triangle of something called "cobbler", a postage stamp of nuclear-hot, apple-flavored goo buried in a puffy spoonful of dough. It was incredibly tempting to have that little dessert right there alongside the dinner, but I never cheated. I saved it for the end so the scalding filling would cool to a non-blistering temperature, when I could savor it without doing any long lasting damage to my tongue. This was, without a doubt, my favorite part of the meal. Just the word cobbler conjured up images in my mind of mothers in flowery aprons carrying oven warm desserts to the table, the scent of cinnamon filling the air. I imagined somewhere in Wisconsin were happy, hearty mid-westerners sitting down to their cobblers every night, and it made me feel wholesome and patriotic to be sharing in this grand American tradition. I would lick the last of the sweet filling out of the corners of the aluminum tray, and then eyeball my brother's dinner in the hopes that he was so preoccupied sticking the buttered peas up his nose that he would forget all about his dessert, and I could make my move. I would wait patiently as Greg systematically denuded his three pieces of fried chicken, stuffing the flakes of batter-dipped skin along with most of the mashed potatoes in his pants pockets, but sometimes he would sneak a pea or two out of his nose and place it in the cobbler, and so effectively dash my dreams of a second helping of dessert.

A loud pop of hot fat jerked me out of my TV dinner fantasy, and I glanced at the clock on the stove. It was still only 11:00 and my mother might not be back for another hour. My stomach let out a low moan and I wished I could transport myself in time, and have that glorious helping of matzoh, piping hot and salty, sitting in front of me on a paper plate. I imagined myself licking up the last of the crumbs and chunky kosher salt from the grease-stained plate, then washing it all down with a glass of my favorite flavor Kool-Aid, which, on this day, happened to be grape. Ah, yes, no finer pairing than grape Kool-Ade with matzoh brei. My salivary glands spurted in happy anticipation, and my empty stomach protested even louder. I looked back at the clock in the foolish hope that time had warped forward, only to be mocked by the slow, creeping second hand. 11:02. I wandered back into the living room. There on TV was yet another animated talking animal in a fedora. I felt nothing but contempt as I watched Yogi Bear running from the park ranger, illicit picnic basket tucked under his arm. But, somehow, on a deeper level, I felt pity. In his eternal quest to fill his belly, wasn't it worth risking his very life for that perfect meal? Why should he be denied, when out there, in the fantasy world of happy families picnicing on gingham table cloths, carefully orchestrated buffets were being spread out for everyone to enjoy? Everyone, that is, except starving, desperate bears. I wished, for once, that Yogi would finally get away with that basket of stolen goodies, and the park ranger would have no choice but to resign, defeated, a miserable failure, unable to keep one lousy bear from stealing nice folk's potato salad.

The Cooking Lesson

By the end of the episode, I, like my hungry ursine counterpart, had begun to accept want as a way of life. I felt my intestines eating themselves, grinding away at nothing in a vain attempt to extract nourishment from gastric juice. I turned away from the television, the sight of Fred Flintstone eating a brontosaurus burger making me sick with envy. I looked out the window, hoping to spy my mother and Greg strolling down White Plains Road, but returned to the couch with resignation. My mother would come home to stir the matzoh when she knew the time was just right, and not a moment sooner. Desperate to not think about it, I wondered instead what she might have planned for dinner.

Thursdays were touch and go, and I could never tell what mood she might be in. If she was still flush with the monthly welfare windfall, she could be feeling generous and send me to the store for some Chun King Chow Mein, a treat usually reserved for birthdays and major holidays. But more often than not, my mother simply couldn't wait for a reason to celebrate something, and Thursdays were almost as festive as Fridays. What better way to live it up than Chinese food in a can! We were such big fans of Chun King, that on the rare occasion when we actually went out to our local Chinese restaurant we were disappointed by the flash cooked broccoli, the crispy carrots and the still-green celery that invaded every dish. I was terrified of the chunks of mystery meat, and the fish with their heads still on, and the vegetable that looked like thinly sliced wood, which my mother warned me had probably been harvested out of the vacant lot behind the restaurant. Why would anyone eat this stuff, when smooth and creamy Chun King was readily available on our grocer's shelf?

I was having visions of my mother pulling the pop-top on the crunchy noodles, and in exquisite slow motion, sprinkling them over the warm, gelatinous vegetables, where they would soften and form a wet, salty blanket, when some drool trickled down my chin and snapped me back to consciousness. My stomach was making sounds like an air raid siren, and I was convinced I would waste away and perish before my mother's return, so I decided I would try my luck at finding something edible in the refrigerator. Nearly delirious with hunger, I pushed aside old cottage cheese containers growing neon orange sludge and furry green lawns. There was a pot my mother had borrowed from Mrs. Krantz last spring, and I wondered if it might have been sitting there all this time. I pulled the pot out, hoping to find maybe some leftover spaghetti from the not too distant past, but the lid stayed glued shut, despite my best efforts to pull it off. I whacked it a couple of times with the wooden spatula, but the lid refused to budge. Putting the pot in the sink, I placed the faucet over it and ran the hot water, and I wrestled with the lid once more, holding on to the fantasy that my efforts might be rewarded with some slightly crusty Kraft Dinner. The hot water splashed and sloshed out of the sink as I pounded the lid, and at last, it gave way, revealing a partially eaten green rectangle stuck to the bottom by some brown cement. Out of morbid curiosity, I pried the rectangle loose with the spatula, and upon closer examination, realized it was part of an old grilled cheese sandwich. Sometime in the distant past, my brother had ditched his half eaten lunch into the pot, along with the last of his milk and coke, and stored it safely away in the back of the fridge. Clever boy! Naturally, I dropped the rancid sandwich back in the pot, closed the lid, and stuck it back in the refrigerator, buried safely behind all the other moldering leftovers.

    Desperation drew me back to the pan on the stove. I was hypnotized by the sheer beauty of the thing. What was once raw and revolting had become captivating in its otherworldly magnificence, a humble combination of fat and carbohydrates, the basic stuff of life transformed into perfection. It called out to me, "Evie…I am yours…just one bite. No one will know." I reached for the spatula, intent on scooping out a small piece, just enough for a forkful, but guilt stayed my hand. My mother would know, and I would be ashamed. How could I let her down?

I began thinking about what my mother would do when she found my gaunt and lifeless body, slumped in the chair just inches away from the delicious, life-giving pan of matzoh brei. I hoped there would be a big, fancy Catholic funeral, and everyone would be grief-stricken, wishing they had been nicer to me, and not thrown my toys out the window, or forced me to eat canned spinach. I was thinking of making out a will, leaving Greg my Barbie dolls and my half of the Matchbox Raceway, which would serve to make him feel even worse for the shabby way he treated me, but I was too weak. I felt sorry for myself, knowing my demise was imminent, and there would be no one there to comfort me as I slipped into the great beyond. I put my head down on the table, and just as I began to well up with self-pitying tears, I heard the scratch of my mother's key in the lock, and, quickly wiping my eyes on my sleeve, leaped up to greet her and Greg.

"Did you touch it?" she asked as she walked into the kitchen, eyeballing the pan.

"No, I swear! Can we eat now?" I practically shouted. I had miraculously recovered from my near-death experience.

"Hold on, would you? I gotta check it first to see if it's ready."

I wondered how, after three hours of frying in molten grease, the matzoh could not be ready, but obviously my mother knew best, and I jiggled with impatience as she took my brother out of the stroller, removed her coat, and lit a fresh cigarette.

At long last, she approached the pan, spatula poised for action.

"Hmmmm....," she said, poking carefully at the edges, testing for firmness with just the right amount of crackle. The tension was palpable.

"OK", she said. "Now it's ready. Watch."

And she plunged in, scooped up a section, then deftly flipped it over. She repeated this procedure, whacking the spatula on the side of the pan each time, until all of it was turned. I tried to absorb the technique, but it all went by so quickly. My vision was going blurry, my head swimming from impending malnutrition, and at that point, I really didn't care about the lesson anymore. I just wanted to eat.

She gave it all a vigorous stir, chopping away with a practiced hand, and finally, turning off the flame, declared the matzoh ready for consumption. I raced to the closet and pulled out the paper plates and kosher salt, and my mother dished out steaming portions for us all. I lost track of time as I stuffed my face, singeing my soft palate, leaving a delicious lava flow of pain down my throat, wishing the plate would never empty. Before long, there was nothing left but a big salty grease spot, which I licked until the paper started to shred.

I sat back, letting out a resounding belch, saved from the ravages of privation, and watched contentedly as my brother methodically stuffed chunks of matzoh down his diaper, my mother taking an occasional bite from her plate in between drags on her cigarette.

"So, what do you think? Are you ready to make it next time?" she asked as she stabbed her cigarette out in the empty plate.

My heart leaped with joy at the prospect! Imagine me, entrusted with the most sacred of cooking secrets, preparing the holiest of holy meals, all on my own! I thought about the day's lesson, the Crisco, and the waiting...the endless waiting. My joy quickly turned to fear and uncertainty. I looked at my mother, searching her face for clues to the right answer. Would she be proud of me if I accepted the challenge, or would she be ashamed that I had not learned well from the valuable lesson? Maybe she needed me to cave under the pressure, and so ensure her rightful place as the High Exalted Queen of Matzoh Brei.

"Nah," I said, after careful consideration. "No one could ever make matzoh like you, mom."

My mother looked at me for a moment, searching my face, and then leaned in closer.

"Yeah, that's what I thought you'd say. Chicken shit," she said and she pushed away from the table and left me alone with three greasy paper plates, a scorched frying pan, and the bitter taste of failure in the back of my mouth.

Olympic Fever

My mother sat at the kitchen table, nervously stirring her cup of instant coffee and eyeballing me intently as I poured a second bowl of Lucky Charms. I had just enough time to pick out the marshmallows and cram them in my mouth and still make it to school on time when my mother said "What's wrong with you?" She leaned forward, her eyes narrowed with suspicion.

"Huh? What do you mean?" I asked.

"You don't look so good. Your lips are green."

"That's just the marshmallow clovers" I answered, wiping the sugary dust from my mouth.

She pushed my bangs aside and expertly applied the back of her hand to my forehead.

"No. You're getting sick. You should stay home. Hurry up, go put on your pajamas before you get any worse!"

"Whatever you say," I sighed, finishing up the last of the breakfast candy. I knew better than to argue with my mother, for she had an almost preternatural talent when it came to detecting illness. She could smell a virus on me before my white blood cells even knew there was an intruder in their midst, and have me bundled up on the couch with a hot water bottle and a box of Luden's before I felt the first pangs of malaise. Without fail, the fever would be raging by the time the morning movie began, and she would kick back and relax with the TV guide and plan out the week's viewing schedule while I succumbed to the ravages of disease.

"Let's see, there's a Steve McQueen flick on Channel Eleven, and then there's a Three Stooges festival this afternoon, and I can't believe it! They're showing The Blob on the Late Show, if you can keep yourself up. Hey, would you mind doing that in the bathroom? How am I supposed to hear the TV over all that goddamn retching?"

My mother's bedside manner left much to be desired, but this is not to say that her nursing skills were shoddy. In fact, she liked nothing better than to have me home with her to watch old movie classics all day, even if that meant straining to hear crucial dialogue over incessant coughing and noisy ejections of mucous. She would pencil in a trip to the family doctor during the afternoon television doldrums, when the only shows on were crappy old reruns of Leave It To Beaver and Father Knows Best, and we would arrive home just in time for the 4:30 movie with a sack of medicinals for me and a fresh carton of cigarettes for her. If we were lucky, there were back-to-back double features, and we barely had to leave the comfort of the television for days on end, while my mother administered doses of antibiotics and cough elixirs to me during commercial breaks. She treated the whole affair like a mid-winter vacation, sleeping until noon and declaring a moratorium on everything from cooking and cleaning to basic hygiene, and we got to eat all the Hostess fruit pies we wanted, while lounging around in our own filth. It was during one of these marathon movie and flu events that my teacher, Miss Kirnan, and my entire fourth grade class showed up at our door. My mother was slightly embarrassed, having neglected to tidy up the apartment since the week-long Hope and Crosby "Road Movie" marathon began, and she reluctantly stepped aside to let the crowd of youngsters and Miss Kirnan come in.

My well-meaning teacher cautiously stepped around piles of greasy pizza boxes, Chinese-food containers and overflowing ashtrays, motioning the children to stay back for safety's sake, and was visibly alarmed when she saw the decrepit state we were all in.

"My God, are you OK?" she asked with genuine concern. None of us had changed out of our pajamas or brushed our teeth in five days, and a damp human smog hung in the air.

"Oh, yeah, yeah, we'll be just fine. She's probably not contagious anymore, but you may want to boil your clothes" my mother advised her, and Miss Kirnan bolted for the door, dropping a pile of get well cards on the floor and shoving my classmates out into the hallway.

"Thanks for coming!" my mother hollered at the fleeing mob.

"Just don't breathe, children. You're all going to be ok!" we could hear Miss Kirnan say, as she ushered the alarmed youngsters down the stairs as quickly as their little feet would carry them.

"How rude of them to just show up like that! Some people have no sense of decency," my mother declared, pushing a heap of snotty tissues off the coffee table to make room for a clean ash tray.

Teachers and classmates alike soon grew accustomed to the fact that I was out sick from school more often than not, and rather than springing more surprise visits on us, polite notes of concern were mailed to our apartment several times a month. My mother would read them aloud:

"Dear Mrs. Levine,

Evanne has been absent 47 times in the past 3 months. We think it would be a good idea for you to come pick up some of her school work so she does not fall too far behind. Blah blah blah!"

She would toss the note in the garbage, having no intention of ever stepping foot inside my school, let alone have an actual conversation with my teacher. Her one hard and fast rule was, 'don't ever make me have to go to your school or talk to your teacher, for any reason, ever, as long as you live'. Authority made her nervous, even sweet, non-threatening Miss Kirnan, with her perky blonde ponytail and her penny loafers.

"What a whore. What is she gonna do, expel you from fourth grade? Like I'm gonna put on a fake smile and listen to your teacher bitch about why it's so important for your 'social and intellectual well-being' to go to school! What the fuck do they know? You'll get more real life skills right here at home than you'll ever get in school. Oh, look, Abbott and Costello Meet Frankenstein is on!"

And so I spent the better part of every winter hanging out with my mother, fighting off one malaise after another, and getting a perfectly decent education in the Art of Slapstick Comedy. That is, until the winter of 1971, when I quite suddenly and without warning, got healthy.

It was sometime between Thanksgiving and Christmas when my mother noticed that I had been attending an unusual amount of school. My first-quarter report card revealed nothing but straight A's, with number of days absent an astonishing "0".

"OK, let's not panic. Maybe you're just saving it all up for one big, terrible infection. We better be prepared. Run to the store and buy the biggest jar of Vicks Vaporub you can find. And some Robitussin. And a carton of cigarettes." My mother was taking no chances. Not once in the history of my childhood had I made it to the holidays without a raging fever and some kind of pox-like illness. My brother had already suffered through colds and boils, strep throat and something like cholera, but I somehow managed to remain well. One morning in early December my mother stopped me as I was preparing to leave for school.

"Was that you I heard moaning? What's wrong, are you feeling sick?" She blocked the front door, shaking the thermometer vigorously.

"No, that was me humming. I feel fine. And I'm gonna be late for school," I said as she pressed two fingers into my neck, checking for a pulse.

She reluctantly stepped aside, warning me of the dangers of cold air exposure whilst harboring deadly, if symptom free, illnesses.

"That's how the Plague started, you know!" she called after me as I bounded down the stairs.

But my mother's warning fell on deaf ears. I made it to school that day, and every day, all the way up to the holidays, and spent an unusual Christmas morning without fever hallucinations and oozing pustules. My mother grew more anxious with every passing diseaseless day, and started worrying that I might actually see a perfect attendance record.

"You'll be sick soon, I just know it" she assured me, but there was a note of panic in her voice as she flipped through her recent Special Edition TV Guide. "Nothing to worry about" she muttered distractedly.

My mother was in fact quite worried, for soon, the greatest television spectacle to come around in years was set to begin, and she was determined to have me at home, sick and miserable and ready to enjoy the entire two week extravaganza that was the XI Winter Olympic Games.

Although none of us enjoyed competition of any kind, and my mother was dead set against anything that smacked of "team spirit," she looked forward to the Olympics with fanatical glee, this despite her generally subversive views on government, organized sports and the so-called benefits of fresh air and exercise.

"You know, you better start taking this seriously, missy" she shook a finger at me. "The trials are beginning this weekend, and I don't think you are anywhere near ready! Look, Channel Four is having the qualifying Downhill event this Sunday, and you're still healthy as a horse. I mean, really, how bad do you want this?"

My mother took to hiding my winter coat beneath the rubble in the toy closet, and sending me off into the frigid January morning with nothing but a light sweater and a frosty bottle of Coke. I would arrive home, all rosy cheeked and robust, ready to head back outside for an invigorating snowball fight with my friends.

"Maybe you should change into your sandals, so your feet don't get too hot?" my mother offered, digging through my drawer for a light pair of shorts and a tank top. "We wouldn't want you to overheat!"

But despite her best efforts, I continued to experience hearty good health with the Olympic opening ceremonies only days away. My mother grew desperate, and decided that a trip to the germ infested pediatrician's office was just what I needed. We arrived at Dr. Schweig's overcrowded clinic, and my mother ushered me over to the "Kontagious Korner," where all the children with hacking coughs and bulging lymph nodes were sequestered behind a cheerfully decorated fortress of Plexiglas. There were flecks of mucous and vomit peppering the walls and in the spaces between the festive paper balloons, and I found myself a seat by a poster showing Harry the Happy Hypodermic holding hands with a grinning penguin. The little girl sitting next to me was blowing green bubbles out her nose, while she snacked on some Oreo cookies, and I instinctively shrank back, holding my breath.

"Hi. By dabe is Bolly. Wad a cookie?" she asked me, dipping her moist fingers into the germ-soaked baggie, a fairly large mucous bubble popping out her left nostril every time she attempted the 'm' sound. I shook my head and pretended to be really interested in Harry's thought balloon: "Inoculations are COOL!"

"Hey, what's wrong with your kid?" my mother asked the sick child's mother

"I don't know. The flu, I guess" she said.

"Great! Why don't you two play together?" my mother prompted, shoving me across the bench to be within easy sneezing distance of the girl. I watched Molly's nose bubble advance, retreat, advance, retreat, and decided I would rather not risk any conversation, fearing one of those bubbles might erupt in my direction. I withdrew to the comfort of a tattered Highlights magazine, and hoped that I might manifest some of my own symptoms by the time my name was called. The bubble blowing girl started looking woozy and she rested her head in her mother's lap, where she promptly threw up her Oreos and began to wail, causing bigger and more voluminous bubbles to emerge and pop, when Nurse Barbara poked her head around the safety wall to call me in. I was only too happy to meet with the dreaded Dr. Schweig, just to get away from the sight of all that snot. Nurse Barbara showed us into a curtained cubicle, had me change into a gown, and I sat myself down on the papered table. The crunch of it under my butt was enough to make me believe that I might actually be sick, but alas, when Dr. Schweig came in, deadpan and scary in his starch stiff coat, I couldn't even muster up a little phlegm.

"Well, now, Mrs. Levine, I haven't seen Evie in some time. What brings you here today?" he droned, looking at the chart that listed my vague symptoms. "You say she's got ear wax? Is she in pain?"

"No. Not really. Well, maybe. Does she need to be in pain to get a doctor's note? I mean, if it was a really bad case of ear wax, could she stay home from school for two weeks?"

"Mrs. Levine, ear wax is not a disease" he said, and he took his pointy little instrument and stuck it in my shiny pink ear canal. "There's nothing wrong with your daughter's ears" he sighed.

"Well, she also has a fungus. Yes, a terrible fungus. I think it might be highly contagious. It's all over her toenails."

Dr. Schweig examined one of my feet and rubbed his forehead as if in pain.

"This is not a fungus. This is black magic marker."

"Oh. So, do you think that's dangerous? What if the ink gets into her bloodstream? I mean, blood poisoning, come on!"

"Is there really something wrong with Evie, Mrs. Levine? I have an office full of sick children out there."

"Yes! We want to get her one of those shots that prevents something really bad, but can make her feel crappy right away. Do you have anything like that?"

Dr. Schweig shook his head and pulled aside the curtain, revealing my flu ravaged bench mate in the next cubicle.

"Go home, Mrs. Levine" he said, "and come back when she has a real problem that I can treat," at which point, bubble girl belched and vomited what was left of her Oreos all over Dr. Schweig's shoes.

We trundled home through piles of black snow and ice, my mother complaining bitterly about Dr. Schweig's obvious lack of diagnostic skills and secret Nazi affiliations, while I frolicked in the mountains of frozen slush.

"That man is pure evil. How could he turn away a child in need? Just look at you, you're practically at death's door. Now come down from there, you'll get piles!"

I slid down the icy slope on my butt and let my mother have her rant, feeling mildly disappointed that I wouldn't get to see the bulky East Germans muscle their way through Luge competition, but mostly sad that we wouldn't get to share those special moments, like when downhill skiers went hurtling like ragdolls through flimsy slalom gates, smashing bones and Olympic dreams alike.

"It's OK, mom. Maybe I'll be sick for the summer games."

"It's just not the same!" she cried, choking back tears.

By the time the opening ceremonies began that Thursday night, my mother had given up hope. We watched the parade of athletes and the glorious images of far-away Sapporo on our tiny black and white television, but she was bitter, refusing to even make fun of the Canadians and their sensible hats. I tried to cheer her up by pointing out that the manliest men were on the women's Soviet ski team, but all the joy was gone for her. She had waited four long years for this, and Fate had dealt her an unfair hand.

"Go to bed now, you have to get up for...school" she whimpered, and off I went to tuck myself in, and before long, the soothing strains of Fanfare for the Common Man lulled me to sleep, while my mother sat alone on the couch in the dark, clutching her trusty TV Guide to her bosom.

I got up the next morning and shuffled into the kitchen for breakfast, and there sat my bleary eyed mother at the table wearing the same clothes she had on the night before, cradling her usual cup of Nescafe and that week's tattered and dog eared TV guide.

"So, I guess you're off to school?" she asked. I nodded and yawned, reaching for the box of Cocoa Crispies.

"Well, I have something to tell you" she said. "I lied. You're not going to miss the Olympics. They're broadcasting it live at night, and none of the good stuff is even going to be on during the day." She looked ashamed.

"Really?" I said.

"Yeah, really. I guess it was just a mother's selfish dream to want her child at home, fighting off an upper respiratory infection together. Is that too much to ask? I guess you just didn't want it as bad as I did. So, go ahead. Go to school, get good grades, see if I care. And here..." she reached behind her and pulled my winter coat out from under a pile of old furniture in the toy closet. "Now go get yourself ready," she said, tossing the coat at me. And in that moment, I felt terrible that I had denied my mother this one small thing, and wished that I could do something to make it up to her.

"OK," I said, and walking around the back of her chair, I gave her a hug and said, "Thags, Bob." And as I said it, and a well formed green bubble emerged from my left nostril for just a brief moment before popping on her cheek, bringing a grateful smile to my mother's face, and a tear of joy to her eye.

Olympic Fever

Waiting For Bunnies

My palms were sweating as I walked distractedly down bustling Allerton Avenue, keeping pace with my mother and her long, gangly stride. It was a rare occasion for my mother to accompany me anywhere, but today was a rare day, and our journey was one ripe with purpose. I looked around at the familiar storefronts, passing by all my usual stops without a pause. The neon Hebrew National sign buzzed and blinked in the window of the kosher deli, and the intoxicating smell of grilling hot dogs and spicy brown mustard wafted out onto the street, but I walked past without a second glance, not even bothering to beg my mother for a quarter to buy an ice cold egg cream at the corner candy store. I barely noticed the deafening thunder of the number 2 train as it came to a grinding halt over our heads. Our destination was a mere block and a half away, but I felt as if I had left all that was mundane and ordinary far behind, bravely venturing forth into new and uncharted waters. I was nervous, but I was ready, so very, very ready. For today was the day that I had dreamed about, agonized over, and even made deals with God for. Yes, today was the day I would get my very first bra.

My odyssey began the day before, a day like any other day, with no hint that anything unusual or earth shattering was about to take place. I made my way home from Frank Whalen Junior High, thinking it would be a good idea to stop for a coke and a slice of pizza to help me forget the torment I had endured at the hands of my soul destroying, masochistic eighth grade math teacher, Mr. Karp, who took great delight in reading my abysmally bad algebra test scores aloud to the entire class. "EVANNE!" he had boomed, "TWENTY SEVEN!" at which point he threw a well aimed eraser at my head with his big, meaty ham hock hand. I still had some chalk dust in my hair as I bit into the luscious, cheesy slice, folded just so, New York style, and scalding, greasy sauce squirted down my shirt. A long slug of icy Coke cooled the burn on the roof of my mouth and I became contemplative, even letting go of my oft replayed fantasy involving Mr. Karp's charred remains being pulled from the flaming wreckage of Frank Whelan Junior High. I walked home sated and at peace, burping garlic.

My mother greeted me at the door, smoldering butt planted in the corner of her mouth. The wooden pasta spoon was still steaming, as she waved it in my direction.

"Where you been? And what the hell are those?" she said, nodding at my ruined tee shirt, squinting through the cigarette smoke.

"What? I just got a slice. I spilled a little sauce, I guess" I said, dropping my backbreaking arm load of text books on the kitchen table.

"No, not the sauce, for chrissake. THOSE..." she said, poking the hot spoon into my shirt, and looking down, I beheld a startling sight: a pair of bee sting-like protrusions. I felt heat rising up my neck, burning my cheeks and evaporating all the saliva in my mouth as I looked incredulously at the tiny bumps interrupting the normally featureless plain of my cotton tee. My hands started to shake.

"What do I do? WHAT DO I DO?" I shouted at my mother, clutching my shirt for fear that these precious gifts might just suddenly disappear and leave me flat chested once again if I didn't take immediate action.

"Well, for starters, you go change out of that dirty shirt, and then you can go buy me a pack of Marlboros. After that, we'll see. Maybe tomorrow I'll take you to Joe Tuckman's for a training bra."

Could it be? This was like a dream come true, like hitting the lottery! I had envisioned this moment a thousand different ways, and every one of those visions ended with me in a plunging V-neck cardigan, showing just enough of my perfect cleavage to Frankie Rao, who was dumbstruck in love with me and powerless against my charms.

My mother took a final drag off the cigarette, crushed the filter into a red plastic ashtray, and aimed her exhalation out the side of her mouth, all the while regarding my stained and lumpish shirt with a look of amusement.

"What do ya know? You're getting bunnies!" she exclaimed.

"What is Evie getting! Am I getting some! Can I have some!" came my brother's shrill and tremulous voice from the bedroom.

I bolted for the bathroom feeling a mixture of elation and nausea. I locked the door and, pulling the shirt over my head, stood in front of the medicine cabinet and stared at the pale pink malted milk balls that had erupted overnight. I turned to the side, hoping they might look more like actual breasts from a different perspective, but they just sat there, rubbery and pointy and decidedly unvoluptuous. I jumped up and down a little bit to see how they would react, but again, I was disappointed when they refused to bounce or relax or jiggle even slightly. In fact, their attentiveness was making me uneasy, so I covered up with a towel and slipped out of the bathroom, hoping Greg wouldn't notice me as I ran into the bedroom to put on a clean shirt. I hastily grabbed a pink tank top and pulled it on just as Greg came up behind me.

"What are you doing!" he bellowed at me from a mere arm's length away, his voice penetrating and accusatory.

"Nothing!" I shrieked back, and ran for the kitchen, my arms folded across my chest. Grabbing the dollar bill my mother had left on the table, I bolted out the door and slammed it behind me, cutting Greg off mid sentence. "Mommy said you have bunnies! Mommy said..!" and I was off down the stairs, eager to be away from the sound of his voice. I was feeling on edge as I crossed Allerton Avenue on my way to old lady Anna's for my mother's smokes, when I caught a glimpse of myself in the storefront window running to make the light. There I was, a hot pink streak flashing my way across the street, and there were my new gumball breasts loudly announcing their presence amidst glitter and fancy script. I had foolishly chosen my "Disco Mama" shirt, and one swollen nipple poked perfectly through the capital "D." I ducked into Anna's, regretting my hasty wardrobe selection, dreading the long walk of shame back home. I made my purchase, waited until I saw the light turn green, and then I ran for all I was worth, clutching the tiny brown bag of cigarettes to my chest. Even in my haste, however, I couldn't help but notice that all around me were women of every age, shape and size, shopping and pushing baby strollers, casually making their way down the busy street. Suddenly I was aware that breasts were everywhere! How did I not notice them before? I tried not to stare, but the variety was endless, and I marveled at how different they all looked. They stuck out in random shapes, spherical, triangular, high and tiny, long and low. They bulged, they sagged, they swelled and swung. What would mine look like? Could it be that these ridiculous little nuggets would one day fill up a sweater? None of the women even seemed to notice that they had breasts. Some were so huge they could barely be contained by even the most gargantuan bras, and great portions had managed to escape from their confines, straining against the fabric and creating mysterious new bulges. I wondered how these women had the nerve to leave their homes. I was in awe of them, and wondered if I would ever feel as comfortable as they seemed to be, walking down the street with these lumps and bumps sticking out for all the world to see. I hunched over my folded arms, feeling embarrassed about my meager offerings, and hurried home to check and see if they had grown at all.

Later that night, I made my way back to bed from yet another trip to the bathroom mirror, convinced that I was doomed to have pointy nubs that would never resemble anything like real boobs. They looked like swollen pencil erasers, strange and out of place on my boyish thirteen-year-old body. I thought about all the beautiful women I wished I looked like, and Jane Fonda in "Barbarella" immediately came to mind. My friends and I were too young to see it at the Allerton Movie Theater, but we all clustered around the poster in the showcase window to gawk at Jane in her skin-tight, space age, plastic-and-metal sheath, which left nothing to the imagination. I was a little embarrassed by Jane's blatant eroticism and shocked by the mass hysteria it created amongst all the boys, who couldn't have been more appreciative, and it occurred to me that as far as they were concerned, boobs were even better than laser guns. I remembered feeling jealous, how I yearned to be the object of such appreciation! Now I was confused and consumed with doubt. I ducked my head under the sheets and picked my pajama top up. They were still there, sticking up like two ant hills. I tried to push them together and create a little cleavage, but they didn't budge. I closed my eyes and conjured up images of my body ideal. Top on my list was Raquel Welch in "One Million B.C." I had recently watched it with my mother one Saturday afternoon, and I was transfixed by her animal sexiness in that fur bikini.

My mother spent the whole movie complaining about how dopey it was, and how could anybody actually believe there were people around a million years ago fighting dinosaurs, and how Raquel Welch was just all fake top to bottom, fake cheekbones, fake chin, fake boobs, while I sat there praying with all my might and making every deal with God, including being nice to Greg and brushing my teeth every night instead of just wetting the toothbrush and not stealing loose change from my mother's beaded purse, if only He would give me boobs like Raquel Welch's. I even dreamed that night that I woke up in the morning to find I had grown a pair of perfect breasts, and my mother had bought me a fur-lined bra, and every boy in the neighborhood wanted to marry me. When I told my mother about the dream, she said "Why are you so obsessed with tits, for chrissake?"

    I thought I had every right to be obsessed. While all my girlfriends were getting their bra straps snapped by randy pubescent boys, I sat forlornly by, the object of no one's wanton lust in my Hanes, girl's white cotton tee. When we played Run, Catch and Kiss in the park, I would claim to have a strained ankle and opt to have a swing instead. It was obvious who was going to get chased and kissed, and it was never the fat girl, or the girl in the coke-bottle glasses, and certainly not the flat chested girl. We would group together, the unsexy ones, and talk about how dumb Run, Catch and Kiss was anyway, as we pumped our legs, straining to push ourselves higher, finding what joy we could in watching our feet touch the sky as our shapelier, prettier, chestier girlfriends got knocked down in the grass and pretended to fight off eager suitors who frantically planted sloppy kisses on or near their mouths, sometimes with tongue, as they clumsily tried to cop a feel. I did my best to ignore the girls' mock cries of distress, and pretended not to care. But I did care, and at the end of the day, as we all walked home together, I listened to tales of who had the best kissing technique, who got passed a piece of "abc" gum mid kiss, what boys were bold enough to attempt a grope. The most desirable girls picked dead leaves out of their hair, brushed grass stains off their jeans and loudly chewed their used gum, snapping and blowing bubbles. I would trudge up the stairs to the apartment, wondering what those kisses felt like, if a boy would ever want to kiss me like that, terrified that Frankie Rao would chase me, kiss me, stick his hand under my shirt and find nothing there to grope.

When I expressed my dismay to my mother, she tried to allay my fears with some sage advice.

"Listen, all those girls wearing bras now are going to have saggy tits by the time they're eighteen. Besides, real women don't wear bras anymore," she proclaimed. She was, of course, referring to the bra burning trend of the late 60's, which freed women of all ages and cup sizes to unburden themselves of those terrible, binding constraints and flop to their heart's content. My eyes drifted down to the area of my mother's chest where most women sported breasts in some way, shape or form, and remembered a time when I was much younger and had the unfortunate experience of walking in on my mother fresh out of the shower. My eyes were immediately drawn to a pair of flabby undercooked pancakes with nipples the size of tea cup saucers, and I ran out of the room crying. My grandmother, whose house we were living in at the time, came to my aid, and folded me into her warm, generous embrace.

"What's the matter?" she said, squeezing me tight against her plentiful 40D's. It felt so safe there, lush and fleshy, the way an embrace should feel.

"Mommy's bunnies are squashed!" I wailed. "What happened to mommy's bunnies?"

"There, there. Don't be scared. Mommy simply doesn't have the common sense to wear proper underwear" she said. My grandmother was a firm believer in the "18-Hour Cross Your Heart Bra", the Sherman Tank of under garments, and I rested my head against her full, overflowing cleavage, trying to forget the terrifying image of my mother's scrawny, naked body.

In reality, it wasn't her fault. My mother had come into this world with all the feminine attributes of a box of pencils. She was the spit and image of my grandfather, bony and tall, curveless and angular. Her nonexistent butt was the perfect bookend to her skeletal chest, no trace of the prominent "shelf" behind or the Rubenesque bosoms my grandmother brought to the gene pool. When my mother hugged me, it was like being poked with sharp sticks.

Images of my mother's scrawny angularity and my grandmother's full curves flickered through my mind as I lay in bed that night, wondering what cup size the Hand of Fate would deal me, trying hard not to run back to the bathroom to check on their progress one last time. I stared at the ceiling, my hands resting atop the new lumps. Their shape felt strange and unfamiliar under my palms. Eventually, dreamy images of Raquel Welch and Jane Fonda running in slow motion through golden wheat fields, as their perfect fur-and-metal-clad breasts bounced in the sunlight, ushered me closer to sleep, and I rolled over onto my stomach as I always did, the tender soreness reminding me they were there. I prayed I would still have them when I woke up the next day.

Sure enough, the next morning found me in front of the bathroom mirror, scrutinizing, pushing and prodding, jiggling while I brushed my teeth, bouncing as I combed my hair, pulling my shirt tight around my chest, reliving the thrill and embarrassment over and over. I could barely contain my excitement at the thought of strapping myself into a magnificent Playtex bra and the wondrous, magical effect it would have on my social life. I would be the envy of my girlfriends, and all the boys would be vying for my attention. I might even be approached by a modeling agency, such would be my perfect transformation. I was lost in thought, practicing my best smile, angling my body to get a good view of my perfect chest and imagining myself posing for Teen Beat with David Cassidy, when my brother pounded on the bathroom door, causing me to scream and send my plastic tortoise shell comb flying.

"WHAT DO YOU WANT?" I shrieked.

"Mommy says it's time for you to go buy your bwah! What's a bwah? Why do you need a bwah? Evie needs a bwah!"

"SHUT UP!" I growled, pushing past him while making sure I kept one arm crossed over my chest.

"What's the matta? What's unda your shirt? Where are you going? Can I get a bwah? Why can't I have one?" my brother prattled on and on. I stood impatiently by the door with my back to him, pretending to examine the peep hole and ignoring his endless stream of queries, when my mother finally announced her readiness and, grabbing Greg by the hand, we made our way downstairs. It occurred to me that this would be the last time I walked these hallways in an undershirt, and I imagined how it would feel to be walking back up the stairs, looking splendid in my new bra, transformed like the once ugly duckling now turned beautiful swan. My mother stopped at the Kessler's door and asked if they wouldn't mind watching Greg for a little while. We turned to go and I could hear Greg regaling Mr. Kessler with the details of my private journey as we made our way down the hallway and out the door. "Evie needs a bwah! Evie has bunnies and needs a bwah! Mommy says I don't need a bwah 'cause I'm a man and I have peanuts instead! Do you have peanuts?" The heavy front door banged shut, muffling the irritating sound of Greg's voice, and I knew I would never be able to look Mr. Kessler in the eye again, but none of that mattered now. I had a date with destiny.

Moments later, we approached Joe Tuckman's, a store half a city block long and packed with enough textiles to clothe all of western civilization. My heart started to pound.

I'd been shopping here many times, but never before did it seem so glamorous, so filled with promise! We stepped inside and made our way through apparel-clogged aisles, passing the familiar racks of jeans and pea coats, flannel shirts and house dresses, and headed straight for the back, where Ladies Lingerie was wedged between Hosiery and Sundries. I spied a familiar kid on my way to the back corner shopping with his mom. He was busy trying on a pair of Converse All Stars, and I caught the smell of fresh rubber as I passed. I was hoping he wouldn't see me as I ducked between great bins of tube socks and Spaldeens, but he caught my eye and I felt my cheeks flame up. My mother kept a lookout for the saleslady, who was next to impossible to find given the overcrowded conditions, while I made my way around garment racks crammed with Maidenform bras. Some of them were so big I could have fit my head inside one cup. I was deep in thought, trying to imagining what such a breast might look like, when a short, rotund woman with a tape measure draped around her neck appeared from behind an adjacent rack loaded down with tent sized bloomers. Her nametag said: "Gladys".

"Can I help you ladies?" she asked, peering up at my mother over the top of her bifocals. Gladys was fairly well endowed, and I wondered what kind of terrible, utilitarian bra she was wearing, as her boobs were slung quite low but shot straight out like a couple of canoes.

"Yeah, she needs a bra," my mother nodded towards me, and Gladys, wasting no time, waddled my way and expertly whipped her tape measure around my chest before I even knew what was happening. I had the sudden sensation that every eye in the store was on me as Gladys pulled the tape snug around my nascent buds, and then she was done. She whipped the tape back around her neck, gave me a quick once over and declared "28AA, right over here." She snatched a miniscule training bra off the rack and held it up for my approval. I was still in shock over the public measuring, and barely had time to gather my wits before my mother and Gladys ushered me back to the fitting room and sent me in to try the thing on.

A training bra is not a complicated thing, but I felt overwhelmed and unsure how to proceed as I beheld the almost nonexistent cups, the adjustable straps, and the three vertical rows of hooks and eyes. I took my shirt off, feeling vulnerable and self conscious, and then attempted to pull the bra on over my head, only to find myself hopelessly entangled. After a few minutes, my mother impatiently called from outside the changing room curtain, "So?" I explained that I was having some trouble, and the next thing I knew, Gladys was there, untangling the mess I had made, positioning the cups, tightening the straps, adjusting the hooks, and then she was gone before I even had a chance to feel mortified that a total stranger had seen my nakedness.

I beheld my new look in the full length mirror, and tugged at the elastic digging into my ribs. The "V" of the bra created the illusion that something breasty was actually going on, and I stared for a few more minutes, turning to the side, leaning over, raising my arms behind my head, wondering what Frankie Rao would think if he could see me now. Then I put my shirt on. I was hoping they might look fuller, rounder, heavier, but they just looked a bit less pointy. There were lumpy fabric folds under my shirt where there should have been some fleshy fullness, and because I didn't have enough to fill up the cups the little bra sagged at the edges. I considered taking it off, but my mother started hollering that I should stop examining myself and hurry it up so we could go home. I walked out of the dressing room, feeling hot embarrassment color my face, the strange binding sensation around my chest and over my shoulders reminding me of the bra's undeniable presence. We made our way to the register, where the Converse boy and his mom were making their purchase. I looked down at his spanking new white sneakers, which looked huge against his scrawny teenage frame, and watched as he shambled towards the front of the store, when one giant shoe caught on the floor and made that terrible squeak of rubber against tile. He looked back in the hopes that no one had noticed and saw me watching him. I may have imagined it, but I was sure his eyes dropped to my shirt front before he flung himself against the door and lunged his way up Allerton Avenue. I stood next to my mother as she paid for my bra, and I glanced down at my chest. There it was, slightly lumpy, moderately uncomfortable, and totally obvious. My mother grabbed the bag containing the little white plastic hanger that I would never use, and we made our way out of the store. I looked up and down the street, halfway hoping we might pass the boy in the new sneakers. Maybe he was hoping to catch another glimpse of me. I watched myself walking in the reflection of every storefront window, studying how different my silhouette looked. I was sure that every person I passed was looking at me and thinking, My! How awkward that girl looks in that bra! Would my friends think the same thing? Would Frankie Rao find me not so much irresistible as hilarious? Suddenly I regretted every deal I ever made with God. Suddenly, it all felt so wrong. My mother was right, why did it matter so much to me? I didn't even want to be wearing the stupid thing. I wanted to be back home in my Hanes girls' tee-shirt playing Matchbox cars with Greg and never have to worry about straps and hooks and cup sizes and lumps in my shirt. We turned the corner and headed up Cruger Avenue, where thankfully, everyone was home having lunch, and as we climbed the stairs in our building I felt an unexpected wave of disappointment. Maybe I wanted Frankie Rao to see me in my new bra after all. Maybe he would think I looked desirable and not ridiculous, and all my wishing and praying and bargaining with God was worth the effort. I was wracked with confusion as we stopped to collect Greg from the Kesslers' where I could hear him still babbling

Waiting For Bunnies

on and on about nothing in his nerve shattering tones. We headed upstairs, and I tried my best to ignore Greg's volley of annoying questions concerning where we went and what we did and did I know that Mr. Kessler also had peanuts and could I show him my new bwah? I headed straight for the bathroom, where I took off my shirt and stood in front of the mirror in my Maidenform Teen Training Bra size 28AA. Maybe it was a trick of the light, but I swore they looked a bit fuller. I noticed that the bra had a little bow in the center, and its clean white fabric practically glowed, giving the impression that I had a tan. I had to admit, I was feeling kind of glamorous. I was imagining Frankie Rao watching me, longing for me, feeling bad about all the times he had ignored me. I gave Frankie a come-hither look in the mirror.

"Hi Frankie" I whispered, leaning in closer. I could hear my brother outside the door, rambling on about something, jiggling the door handle, but all I could think about was Frankie Rao secretly watching me, and finding me incredibly attractive.

"What do you want to do, Frankie?" I asked my reflection. "Do you want to play Run, Catch and Kiss?" Greg was getting agitated, his voice reaching new levels of hysteria, his little fist pounding on the door.

"What are you doin in theah Evie? Mommy said you betta come out! Mommy said you have bunnies!"

"Want to catch me, Frankie?" I said, moving in closer.

"Evie! I have peanuts! Do you have peanuts?!"

"Do you want to kiss me?" I asked Frankie Rao. "I have something you may want." I leaned over, pushing the little molehills together, so Frankie could get a good view.

"EVIE! WHY ARE YOU IN DA BATHROOM? EVIE! WHY CAN'T I HAVE A BWAH?"

"OH MY GOD! WHY CAN'T YOU LEAVE ME ALONE?" I screamed.

"Evie, mommy said you have bunnies. I don't have bunnies 'cause I have peanuts."

"I KNOW ALREADY!" I shouted at him.

"Will you come out and play Matchbox cars?"

"NO!"

I heard him putter away, shouting to my mother that I was in the bathroom with the bunnies, and Mr. Kessler said that only girls had bunnies but Mr. Kessler had bunnies AND peanuts and why didn't I want to play Matchbox cars with him? I partially caught my mother's response from the kitchen through the bathroom door, which entailed a disclaimer regarding Mr. Kessler not having actual bunnies and also why I may not want to play Matchbox with Greg at this moment in time due to obsessive pubescent narcissism. Looking back at myself in the mirror, I noticed that one of the straps had loosened a bit, and the already mostly empty cup sagged dispiritedly. I threw my shoulders back to improve the view again, but it was more effort than I cared to give, and I slumped forward with a sigh and pulled my shirt back on, the droopy cup puckering beneath. I sat on the toilet, listening to the distinctive sounds of a game of stickball starting up in the street, shouts and curses and the occasional crack of stick against Spaldeen reverberating off the brick buildings. Frankie Rao would surely be out there, and I contemplated going outside. I jumped up to reexamine myself in the mirror one more time, hoping that there had been some sort of dramatic change in the past 30 seconds and immediately abandoned the idea, thinking it might be better to just pretend to have an upset stomach and stay locked in the bathroom for the rest of the day. Out in the living room, Greg and my mother were assembling the Matchbox race track and arguing over who got to be the blue car, my mother insisting that red made her nauseous because of a guy she went out with who drove a red car that she threw up in, which served him right anyway, while my brother whined that red was only for girls and he should be blue because he was a man and if Mr. Kessler had peanuts AND bunnies what color car would he be? My mother was avoiding revisiting the topic by telling Greg to shut up and pick a goddam car, when I came out of the bathroom and tried to slip past them and into the bedroom without being noticed.

"Hey, are you done examining your self or what?" my mother queried.

"Yeah, Evie, what were you doing? We're gonna play Matchbox. You can be wed because you are a girl!" Greg shouted gleefully, and picking up the yellow car, licked the roof and grimaced.

I walked into the living room and stood in front of my mother, who sat cross legged on the floor. "Can you tell?" I asked as she lit a cigarette with one hand while wrestling the blue car out of Greg's clammy little hands with the other.

"Tell? What, that you're wearing a bra?" she asked, and I nodded. "Yeah, you can tell" she said.

"But do I look...booby?" I said under my breath.

She exhaled loudly, and said "Isn't that the point?" and with a final tug, freed the blue car from my brother's grip, and wiped it dry on her pants leg.

"I...guess" I said, and watched as the little cars went zipping around the figure 8. I could hear the raucous sounds of the stickball game coming from the street, in full swing now.

"So? Why don't you go out and show them off already?" my mother said, muscling the blue T-Bird past Greg's yellow Mustang, which went careening off the tracks and smacking into the wall. "CWASH!" Greg screamed with delight, as he retrieved the tiny car parts that had been ejected on impact. I resisted the urge to laugh, and glanced longingly at the unwanted red car. Outside, two of the boys were engaged in a lively dialogue about each other's mothers.

"Maybe later" I said, heading towards the bedroom, where I took off my new Maidenform Training bra and stuffed it under my pillow, and lay on the bed, listening to the boys playing in the street, hoping and praying to God that by dinnertime, I would have something more to show off to Frankie Rao, something like Raquel Welch in that fur bikini, something really, really worth waiting for.

Waiting For Bunnies

Tasteless

After years of Friday night "dates" and clandestine phone calls from Ma Bell telephone booths, my mother's boyfriend, Batman, left his fed up and increasingly dangerous wife and moved in with us. Well aware of Batman's infidelities, his wife had started making it a habit to express her rage while he slept, enabling her to do things to him that would have been prohibitive had he been awake, such as setting fire to his shorts (while he was wearing them), and stabbing him in the neck with a fork. Eager to get some shut-eye in a less hostile environment, his only recourse was to pack up his toothbrush and relocate to our tiny hovel. It was a big adjustment for all of us, as my brother and I tried to adapt to having a man in the house, and he tried his best to ignore us, perhaps hoping that we might go away.

Batman left behind two strapping young sons, who, like their dad, enjoyed watching football and used the word "ain't," two activities that were strictly frowned upon in our house, but they quickly became a regular part of our daily existence. Gone were those cozy nights with The Waltons and The Bradys as Batman made it clear that any televised sporting event meant the rest of us could spend the evening rereading old Mad magazines and Archie comics outside of his field of vision, as our presence might cause an interruption in his enjoyment of the game.

"If you ain't gonna watch the game, then go to your room so I don't have to hear youse two reading," Batman would suggest.

We usually took heed of this advice, as before long, large and potentially dangerous objects, like shoes or beer cans, would go hurling across the room, missing the TV screen by mere inches. I hated to think what would happen if our raucous reading distracted him.

My mother was thrilled to have her boyfriend move in, but besides enforcing the changes in our television viewing habits, Batman also came with some rigorous dietary demands. Fried Spam and Cracker Jacks was not his idea of an acceptable family dinner, and my mother struggled to put meals on the table that received Batman's approval. Having been raised by an immigrant Italian family, he was used to traditional Mediterranean cuisine, and he insisted that my mother learn how to cook what he considered to be real food.

"Judi, when I get home tonight, I want some chicken parmesan. Not that fried crap you get from that fucking shit hole take out place. I want real chicken, like my mother makes, not no fucking moolie chicken."

By "moolie chicken," our new live- in father was referring to the establishment on Boston Road that featured deep fried chicken parts and a variety of artery clogging side dishes, a place often frequented by people of color and welfare folk, such as ourselves. It happened to be one of my mother's favorites, but that was all in the past. Batman wanted chicken like his mother made it, and my mother was eager to provide it. Taking a deep breath, she put her one and only frying pan on the stove, a look of steely resolve on her face. She then took stock of our pantry ingredients, and burst into tears. In a panic to have his dinner ready when he arrived home from work, she disregarded Batman's strict instructions and sent me out to Chicken Delight for a family size bucket. Artfully arranging the fried chicken pieces in her ancient aluminum pan, she cleverly covered them all in ketchup and American cheese, hoping Batman wouldn't notice that anything was amiss. But alas, she forgot that it's almost impossible for a mouthful of chicken bones to go unnoticed. After almost breaking his tooth on a tiny femur, Batman expressed his displeasure by throwing the pan across the room, and my mother had the daunting task of learning how to make him a chicken dinner that had not already been batter dipped, deep fried, and stuck in a cardboard box.

It was recommended to me and my brother that we call Batman "daddy," as my mother assumed this would imbue her hard earned prize with a strong familial sense, and make him want to stay in spite of her futile attempts to make anything resembling "food." I took to the moniker quite easily, sensing that Batman did not actually harbor any feelings of resentment or disgust towards me. Greg, on the other hand, was a different story. As the usurper of the male fruit of Batman's loins, my odd and undersized brother had some massive shoes to fill when it came to playing the role of Son. While his own muscular boys were somewhere in glamorous, suburban New Jersey, beating up first graders and growing facial hair before their tenth birthdays, Batman was busy avoiding both conversation and eye contact with Greg whenever possible. In all the time he lived with us, Batman never once called my brother by his actual name, referring to him as "the other one." The only interaction I can ever recall them having was when my brother had removed all the knobs from the television and flushed them down the toilet. Upon discovering the vital missing pieces just as the game was about to start, Batman became enraged, grabbed Greg by the back of the shirt and asked him if he would like to "get an ass kicking," to which my brother replied, "No, thank you."

It's also fair to say that Batman was not much of an animal lover. He took an instant dislike to our cats, banishing them from whatever room he happened to be in with a swift, construction-booted kick. I noticed that when he wasn't around, Py would quietly slip into the bedroom and sit on his pillow, spending hours washing and grooming, dislodging particles of cat litter from between her toes, and ejecting crud from her ears with an energetic flick of the paw. Sensitive to the sound of his heavy footfall, Py would beat a hasty retreat before Batman's key was even in the lock. Many mornings, Batman would come to the breakfast table not knowing his face was dotted with bits of cat effusion, and I was not about to call attention to it. Py foolishly crossed the line one day by leaving a large, well-formed hairball right in the smooth indent on the pillow, right where Batman would rest his cheek, and after a close miss from his steel-toed boot, she prudently found a new spot for her daily grooming routine.

My mother struggled through the years to better her cooking skills in the hopes of keeping Batman from running off to one of the other girlfriends he kept, several of whom undoubtedly knew how to make him a steak that wouldn't cause a dislocated jaw and bleeding of the gums. Even the simplest dishes became marathon events, as my mother remained true to her credo that the longer you cooked something, the better it tasted, which may have been the case had she been roasting a whole suckling pig. But a meatloaf baked for eight hours will always taste like an incinerated football, no matter how much ketchup you put on it. Often, Batman would walk away from his untouched plate and disappear into the night, in search of a dinner that didn't taste like it had been cooked in a house fire. This would prompt my mother to close herself in the bedroom and cry herself to sleep, thus freeing me and my brother up to feast on Devil Dogs and Ring Dings, and watch Sanford and Son to our heart's content.

Life was unpredictable for the next couple of years, as my mother's cooking forays became more desperate, and Batman became less willing to risk his life just for a hot meal. The more time he spent away, the worse she cooked. It almost seemed to be a culinary game of "Chicken," where the winner gets unconditional love, and the looser gets to have his stomach pumped. But make no mistake, my mother did not sit meekly by, quietly waiting for her man to nod his approval. Many dinners were thrown against walls by my mother's own hand, and epic fights of extraordinary length and volume became commonplace. More often than not, these fights would end with Batman packing his toothbrush and leaving with an enthusiastic slamming of the door. My mother would fall into a funk, using up all of our toilet paper to blot her swollen eyes, and she would lie in bed for days as mountains of soggy wads accumulated around her. Greg and I would take advantage of the opportunity to have Cap'n Crunch for breakfast, lunch and dinner while our mother was incapacitated, but unfailingly, Batman would come back and all would be right with my mother's world again, at least until the next disaster.

And so, as luck would have it, that disaster came in the form of an unplanned arrival. In the quiet moments between their ferocious fighting and flinging of tableware, the expectant couple picked out baby names, while making space in the living room to accommodate the crib and a rocking chair accompanied by a standing ash tray. The mother to be was once again reduced to a diet of crackers and table salt, but nonetheless, enjoyed a radiant glow that could only be attributed to the joy of carrying the seed of the great love of her life. My mother knew that nothing would bond her errant beaux to hearth and home better than the gift of a bouncing bundle of his very own genetic material. It was her sure fire equivalent to a shot gun wedding. Baby Nina was born on a blustery cold night and within a few months, Batman had packed his toothbrush for the last time, never to return.

My brother and I were not privy to the events leading up to our stand-in father's departure, having spent the summer at a sleep away camp. My grandmother felt that we needed to breathe some clean, smoke free air for a change, and feel green grass beneath our feet. After six weeks in the fresh mountain air, we came home from Vermont covered with festering mosquito bites, our feet blistered and scarred from having lost our shoes only days after arriving. A month and a half of camp food put the finishing touches on our misery, and I was actually looking forward to the comfort of my mother's home-cooked swill. Greg had the luxury of returning to our grandparent's house, where he would be greeted by a feast that would have impressed Caligula, but I was happy to be going home to Cruger Avenue. I missed my baby sister, and my mother, and even Batman. After spending a whole summer with other disoriented city kids stumbling around smelly barnyards and getting chased by crazed and dangerous farm animals, I was homesick for a warm blast of subway air, the comforting wail of police sirens, even the strange kid who ran the newsstand where I bought my Archie comics who barked like a dog. I couldn't wait to get back to all the sights and smells of home.

I used my key to open the door, coughed my way through a thick cloud of pungent incense and called out to my mother, who emerged out of the fog wearing a Mumu. She threw her arms around me, and a string of Puka shells pressed into my face, leaving painful indentations.

"I have someone I want you to meet!" she exclaimed with uncharacteristic enthusiasm, reeking of Patchouli oil and sweat. My mother took me by the hand and led me into the living room, where loud sitar music played from the stereo, and a young, stringy man sat on the floor in his underwear, my prize steel-string guitar casually draped across his lap. A cigarette clung to his alarmingly-relaxed lower lip, and he smiled wanly up at me.

"Heeeeyyyy…you must be Evie!" he managed to gurgle. I felt the adrenaline squirting out from my kidneys.

"Who's that? And where's daddy?" I asked my mother, trying to keep my eyes from wandering to the young man's urine stained BVDs.

"He's gone" she said matter-of -factly. "This is Jay. You can call him pop."

"Yeahhhh…pop is cool, man!" the semi-naked stranger concurred, strumming a discordant note on the Goya that had been a gift to me from my grandmother. I had the sudden urge to send my farm blistered foot through the delicate body of the guitar, plunging splinters and all into Jay's unprotected sack.

"I'm not calling you pop" I seethed. "And I want my guitar back."

"Yeah, that's cool" Jay said, obviously eager to win me over with his willingness to see things my way, and standing up, stumbled back against the wall, whacking the guitar against his shin. He let out a yelp, and the cigarette dropped from his lip, leaving a trail of sparks down his pale body before landing on his foot. I watched the guitar fall in slow motion, unwilling to move into his naked personal space to try and rescue it, and it smacked onto his big toe before landing string side down with a twang. Jay was busy patting down his crisped chest hair while attempting to massage the injured toe, when he stepped on the still-smoldering cigarette, sending him careening into the television set with a surprised hoot of pain. Stepping over his writhing body, I snatched my guitar and looked over at my mother, who was nursing Jay back to health by placing a freshly lit cigarette between his lips. The sitar music droned on, setting a surprisingly relaxed tone to the disturbing scene playing out before me. I headed to my room, guitar in hand, and turned back to make my dramatic announcement.

"I want Batman back. And don't ever touch my guitar again!"

Jay leaned against the television, cradling his injured foot, while my mother dusted the particles of burnt hair from his chest.

"Yeah, that's cool!" Jay called back.

In spite of making my wishes abundantly clear, Batman never returned, and Jay persisted in molesting my guitar. A self professed music lover, he also made himself quite familiar with my album collection, and most days I would come home from school to find him dancing around the apartment only slightly more clad in filthy jeans and love beads, playing my precious steel string, banging out maddening, off-key approximations of my favorite songs, as they blasted on the stereo. I found ingenious ways to take the joy out of his life by carving messages of hate into the albums he liked most, and breaking the strings on the guitar.

My mother was uninterested in my crude campaign of rebellion, and in fact, seemed to be in a state of chronic relaxation. She stopped stressing over meal time, and she and Jay often spent the dinner hour taking long naps which stretched into the following afternoon. At first, I was just fine with having Coco Puffs and Pepsi for dinner, but soon I was sharing strained peas and baby custard with my little sister. I knew my mother and I needed to have a talk, so one afternoon, I came home from school and roused her out of bed.

"Mom, there's no food in the house, except for some Similac."

"Huh? Oh, wait a minute," she sat up rubbing her sunken eyes. "What about that jar of mayonnaise?"

I explained to my mother that mayonnaise was not necessarily a meal, and that the baby and I needed something more substantial to eat. She told me not to worry, that Jay would take care of it, at which point she kicked his slumbering body out of the bed and onto the floor with a thud. He was in a more advanced state of undress than usual, and from my vantage point, his naked ass looked like a couple of Kaiser rolls.

"Get up. The kid's gotta eat" my mother yelled at his inert form.

I shielded my eyes, and exiting the room, heard him mumble into the floor "Oh, yeah, food. Cool."

Jay took care of the food situation by shoplifting as much stuff as he could fit under his dungaree jacket, and returned to the apartment with a jar of peanut butter, some grape jelly, a loaf of Wonder Bread, and six jars of Gerber Vienna Sausage. My mother enthusiastically slathered the bread, and the two of them wolfed down several sandwiches, apparently quite hungry after not eating for a couple of weeks. I didn't really mind peanut butter, and it was a refreshing change from tap water and cereal dust. I enjoyed my sandwich while watching Nina mash the little pale hot dogs into a paste on her high chair tray. Now that I had a full belly, things didn't seem that bad, and I thought perhaps I had been too hard on Jay. I felt bad for scratching "FUCK YOU" and "DIE" into every Elton John record I owned, and decided to ease up on him. I would show Jay that I could extend the hand of friendship, and it gave me that warm, fuzzy feeling inside to know I was morally superior to the scumbag who was sharing my mother's bed.

But after a few days, the cupboards were bare, and I found myself once again needing to alert my groggy mother to the fact that we had no food. Jay was sent out, only to return once again with peanut butter, jelly and white bread. I was disappointed, hoping he might steal a box of Kraft Dinner or even a jar of Fluff, just to keep things interesting. But my mother attacked the Skippy with great enthusiasm, exclaiming what a stroke of genius on Jay's part to have chosen strawberry jam this time. They prepared their meal with great attention to detail, covering the bread from corner to corner with equal parts of each ingredient, and then stacked their prizes on a paper plate, and disappeared back into the bedroom. I watched them go, and decided that it was not so great being morally superior, and in lieu of a hearty "Bon apetit!" I shouted "I hope you choke on it!"

Several days later, without any prompting from me, I came home to find my mother and Jay in the kitchen, which in itself was a big surprise. They seemed to be very excited about something, and I peered over their shoulders to see what the hubbub was all about.

"Check this out!" my mother exclaimed. "Look what Jay found in the supermarket!" and Jay proudly held up a jar of something called Goober's, which was festively striped layers of, what else, peanut butter and jelly.

"And the really cool thing is, you can either mix them together, like this..." and the delicate process was demonstrated for me, "OR...you can leave the layers separate, and just let them swirl together when you spread them on the bread!"

Oh, happy day! It was like they had just discovered the cure for cancer, and Jay and my mother danced around the kitchen, trying different techniques, more stirring, less stirring, only stirring the top layer, applying an unstirred portion to one slice of bread, and then mixing the rest to create a multidimensional effect.

"Yeah, man, we even have a name for it. We call it... MIXTURE!" Jay was quite proud of his accomplishment, and the young inventors Samba'ed their way back into the bedroom, where they could enjoy the fruits of their labor.

I was determined to boycott this "mixture" in a Ghandi-like gesture of self-sacrifice, to show them I would stand for the suffering no more. I shared a couple of Vienna sausages with Nina, even tried to wash them down with a few sips of Similac, but halfway through Chico and The Man hunger won out over ideals, and by the end of the show I had decided that Freddie Prinze looked a lot cuter on a stomach full of Goober's.

Several seasons came and went, and it was apparent that my mother had no intention of ever cooking again. Mixture became a way of life. Jay emerged from the dark and smoky bedroom every couple of days to throw his patch-covered dungaree jacket over his scrawny white shoulders, and venturing out to the supermarket, would come home with an armload of contraband Goober's. My mother, although becoming alarmingly gaunt, would still greet him with childlike enthusiasm.

"What did you get? What did you get?"

"You'll never believe it…they have super-chunk now!"

"Oh my God!"

They would perform the same ritual, stirring and spreading, extolling the virtues and singing the praises of Magnificent Mixture, pile up the plate, and back to the bedroom they would go. I kept myself busy, taking care of Nina and hanging out with my friends by day, and carving up the remaining albums and gouging holes in the Goya by night. But before long, I came to the conclusion that it was time for a change, and I resolved to talk to my mother before another batch of Mixture could be stirred.

Arriving home from school the next day, I found my mother on the floor, peering under the couch. At first I thought she was looking for a dropped cigarette, or a broken string of Puka shells.

"What's going on, mom?" I asked.

"It's the ducks. I have to get them. I need the ducks." She had a strange and droopy look on her face.

"What ducks?" I asked, glancing around the room.

"My ducks! Hey, who are you?" She stared crazily over my left shoulder, and I knew something was terribly wrong.

"Where's Jay?" I asked her, seeing he was not in the apartment, fairly sure that this was not his regularly scheduled day to shoplift.

"Oh, that guy. He went to get the ducks!" she answered in an irritated slur, and then she turned her head and hocked a loogie on the wall. I felt my head break out in a sweat. Running to the bedroom window, I pulled the blinds open to look out front, and saw Jay making his way across Cruger Avenue on hands and knees. He stopped to examine a piece of dog poop, which he picked up and stuck in his pocket. I did a quick search of the street, hoping that none of my friends were around to witness this scene, but there they were, sitting on our usual stoop, watching Jay having a conversation with a bag of garbage. Heading back into the living room I watched my mother vomit Technicolor Mixture into the plastic potted plant, and realizing what I needed to do, picked up my baby sister and left, locking the door behind me. As I hurried up the street, I avoided making eye contact with my friends, and passing Jay slowly crawling across the road, mumbling and oblivious, I sincerely hoped he would be crushed by a bus.

As it turned out, Jay somehow managed to survive the journey and make his way back upstairs to the apartment, dragging his new bag-of-garbage friend behind him, his pockets laden with the dog turds that he mistakenly took to be rubies and emeralds. My mother had passed out head first in the potted plant, and awoke the next day to a dried vomit facial and the knowledge that her kids were gone. An unapologetic conversation with my grandmother revealed that she and Jay were heroin addicts, and that they had decided to move up to Connecticut, where, unlike cold, heartless New York methadone clinics, Hartford methadone clinics were all warm and cozy and served big plates of homemade cookies, or so she had heard from a junkie friend of a junkie friend, who was an authority on the subject.

Googie hung up the phone and relocated Ernie from the solarium where he was currently entombed in a paisley duvet to the living room couch, and my little sister and

I settled in amongst the dust covered aquariums and the brown and crumbling tropical flora. My grandmother put some clean sheets on the cot, and I went to bed that night with a stomach full of her homemade chicken soup, but I stared out the window at the streetlight for hours, and listened to my grandparents snoring in the next room, feeling secure but strangely unnerved. Slipping out of bed, I tip-toed down to the kitchen in the dark, and looked through the crowded, disorganized closet, breathing in the lovely aromas of dried herbs, pushing past the boxes of cookies and Entenmann's cakes, until I found what I was looking for, and quietly making my way back upstairs, I settled myself between the crisp sheets with the jar of Skippy and a spoon. I cracked open the jar, scooped out a heaping spoonful of peanut butter, and finally fell asleep with my tongue stuck to the roof of my mouth.

Bishop Desmond Tutu the Runt of the Litter

"What are you doing!" my grandmother shrieked, as she stood in the wreckage of what used to be her living room. I had managed to convince my brother to help me do a little "fixing up," now that we were all going to be living together in my grandparents' house, and the first thing I deemed unacceptable was the deep pile carpeting that reeked of my grandfather's favorite Turkish tobacco and many generations of Yorkshire Terrier dams, sires and puppies and the tsunami of excrement they had left behind. My grandparents took a laissez faire attitude when it came to housebreaking their pets, and were happy as long as the dogs didn't pee on the couch or drop their tiny, tootsie roll sized turds in the bed where they lay sleeping. Not surprisingly, the dogs seemed to enjoy the comfort of plush woolen fibers beneath their tiny terrier paws, and had been pooping and peeing freely on the wall to wall for decades.

My first morning as a permanent resident of Googie and Ernie's house, I assessed the situation. I looked around at the handsome trappings my grandparents had surrounded themselves with; the cherry wood escritoire piled with mountains of National Geographics, the chaotically arranged library of classical albums, the gilt framed reproductions of Michelangelo and Picasso crammed into every available inch of wall space. But if I closed my eyes and inhaled deeply, it wasn't hard to imagine myself shackled to a cement wall in a Turkish prison, languishing in a pool of urine. I knew exactly what I had to do, but lacking a team of professional movers, I did the next best thing.

"But I don't want to!" my brother protested. "Think of the wonderful sense of satisfaction you'll get" I said as I twisted his arm behind his back. I enlisted Greg's help the moment my grandmother left for work that morning, knowing there was no way I could move the heavy Mahogany furniture and roll up a half ton of shag carpeting on my own, and so my sixty pound kid brother and I went to work. Later that evening, as my grandmother observed the work in progress, jamming her clenched fist between her teeth, it was obvious that she simply failed to see the big picture. I tried to explain that it was for the comfort and greater good of us all, but she left us to manhandle the twenty foot rug inch by inch out a casement window only two feet wide without so much as a thank you.

My grandmother accepted the idea that my need to redecorate was cathartic and she let me have my way with her house. She gave me carte blanche picking out the new Linoleum, and even let me rearrange rooms to be more ergonomically friendly. But I quickly became dictatorial. Purging the house of unnecessary items like old photographs and legal documents, I embarked on my ruthless campaign to tidy up. And I was not above persecuting family members.

"Are you done with that?" I would bark at my grandfather as he reclined in his Lazy Boy, trying to wrestle the five pound Sunday New York Times away from his grip. "What are you talking about? I just sat down to read it!" he would say.

"Yes, but you don't want to waste your whole day just sitting around, do you?" It would eat me alive to watch Ernie peruse at his leisure, the massive newspaper spread out before him as he took his sweet time with every section, and I would swoop in to angrily gather up the pages he was done with before they hit the ground, making a big show of putting them back in proper order.

"There. Not so hard" I would mutter as I refolded each section carefully, making sure the creases lined up. Ernie would puff on his pipe and let the Business Section slip to the floor while I was still obsessively reorganizing Arts and Leisure.

I became mad with power, and everyone started avoiding me, keeping their things hidden away where I couldn't find them. Ernie retired to his bedroom indefinitely, making an occasional appearance only to fry up a slab of salami and grab a box of Entennman's before beating a hasty retreat back up to his safe zone. "Make sure you throw that box out when you're done. And don't leave the fork in it!" I would yell as he fled up the stairs, clutching the quilt around his head with one hand and his pie with the other.

As if in defiance of my terrorizing reign of neatness, my brother secretly began collecting things with a vengeance, and soon had his room filled with an obscure and seemingly irrational collection of memorabilia and flotsam. Greg would hoard anything with written words, from tomes of archaic "how to" manuals on everything from zeppelin repair to starting your own yak farm, to cereal boxes, junk mail, greeting cards, phone books, flyers, Chinese food menus, cocktail napkins, Bazooka Joe comics, postage stamps, and most especially, anything between two covers, hard or soft, old or new, fine first editions or water logged Jehovah's Witness' Alive! rescued from the stoop. And Greg was not just a bibliophile, he actually read everything he collected. He could spend Saturday morning immersed in Chaucer, follow it up with a pile of Archie and

Jughead comics, and then wash it all down with the latest Washington Week in Review. He would emerge from his room some time around sundown, pale and hungry, still in his disheveled pajamas, only to pause on his way to the bathroom, captivated by a peed-on Pennysaver stuck to the hallway floor.

"Huh. Food Town is having a sale on Green Giant French Cut Green Beans" I would hear him musing from behind my closed bedroom door.

If it was written, Greg needed to read it, and once he read it, he never forgot it. Want to get some Kung Pao chicken at Lucky Chan's? Greg could recite the entire menu, with prices, lunch and dinner. Want to have the inner workings of an atomic bomb explained in layman's terms? Greg was your man. As maddening as it seemed, there was a sort of practicality to his compulsion. And that I could appreciate.

Because I was the hands down favorite of my adoring grandmother, I had free reign over the house and all its contents from the day we moved in. I admired Googie and her hard working ethos, but I simply could not abide her pack-rattish nature, so while she was off to work bright and early every morning, I was busy purging closets of food stuffs from the previous decade and donating sack loads of outdated clothing to The Salvation Army. Googie would come home from a long day of bookkeeping to find her freezer defrosted, the long forgotten pork chops she purchased during the Eisenhower administration pried loose from their glacial moorings. Sock drawers now contained socks instead of tuna fish cans filled with pennies, and knick-knack shelves were emptied of angels, bunnies, doggies, kitties, paper weights and homemade ash trays, and scrubbed down to the wood. My grandmother would "Ooh!" and "Ah!" over the changes, and then she would secretly rummage through the dozens of garbage bags I'd carefully lined up at the curb to retrieve her beloved paint chipped ceramic figurines, moth eaten wardrobes and

Bishop Desmond Tutu, the Runt of the Litter

swollen cans of labeless mystery food. Within a day or two of one of my massive overhauls, the house was right back to its messy, cluttered, overstocked condition, and the freezer would be filled back up to capacity and laboring away to encase everything in a new block of ice. We all found this to be an acceptable arrangement.

As much as she loved me, and perhaps even my siblings, there were two things Googie loved even more, and those were her job and her dogs, in that order. Back in the late fifties, my grandmother managed to secure herself a bookkeeping position at the powerful Council on Foreign Relations in New York City, despite having no bookkeeping experience and some pretty shady political affiliations. By some miraculous oversight of her lack of a college education and her shameless piles of dirty Pinko laundry, the private-membership political group welcomed my grandmother into their elite fold. At the Council she would meet dignitaries and diplomats, presidents and political pundits and, indisputably, some of the biggest brainiacs in the world, and my grandmother felt right at home among them. Our conversations at the dinner table would often begin with casual references like, "So, I was chatting with the prime minister of India today. She seems like an intelligent person, but why would anyone want to live in India, for god's sake? I mean really, who could eat that disgusting food? No wonder they're all so skinny. I told Mrs. Ghandi that it wouldn't kill her to eat a little beef." And, "So, I met Henry Kissinger today. I couldn't understand a single word he said. I said, 'Mr. Kissinger, you really should speak up. How do you expect people to understand you with that accent?" Mr. Kissinger was not amused when my grandmother then plucked a long blond hair from his jacket and clucked disapprovingly

Through the years, many forgotten items left at the Council by busy, important people rushing about to catch private jets made their way back to our house. The front hall closet became a cache of expensive umbrellas, hats, gloves, scarves, overcoats, pashminas, and oddly, one left shoe, which my grandmother claimed belonged to Ronald Reagan. "He took it off to shake a pebble out, and then forgot to put it back on. I saw him walk out the front door in his sock, but I wasn't about to say anything! What am I, his maid?" We enjoyed using all the nice things that would never be returned to their rightful owners, and tossed around phrases like, "Did you happen to see Richard Nixon's earmuffs? It's a little colder out than I thought" and "Does Mrs. Thatcher's cloche go with these Hotpants?"

One particularly beloved item was a deliciously soft cashmere scarf that had belonged to Kurt Waldheim, the Austrian UN Secretary General. We all coveted it for its incredible texture, and I liked to imagine myself a happy little freuline skipping down the charming, frosty streets of Vienna as I wore it on my way to the post apocalyptic reformatory that was Christopher Columbus High school. Not only did it keep me toasty warm, but I swore I could detect the comforting fragrances of beer and bratwurst still clinging to the expensive fabric. My brother and I fought for the privilege of wearing it, and it was a daily battle to be the first to grab the scarf out of the coat closet and run out the door, laughing and taunting the unfortunate sibling who then had to walk to school scarfless and shivering. But one frigid January morning, I tore through the closet and came up empty handed. "Where's the damn scarf?" I demanded, grabbing my brother by his twig like upper arm. In the midst of his outraged denial, my grandmother announced that the scarf was off limits, due to the fact that Secretary General Waldheim had, in fact, been exposed as a Nazi and removed from his post at the UN. "No Nazi scarf will ever touch the necks of my grandchildren!" she screamed in a fury. We begged to know what would happen to the scarf, and Googie informed us it would now be put to better use as a wee-wee pad for the newest litter of Terrier pups. My brother and I bolted to the living room, hoping to save the precious fabric from ruination, but we were too late. There in the whelping box lay Gremlin and her six naked mole rat puppies, all squealing and blind and smelling of dog milk, curled up on a bed of that lush, Hunter Green luxury. My brother and I held back tears as Googie expertly dabbed away some mustardy poo from a pup with one corner of the beautiful hand stitched scarf.

"That's right, my little angels. Nothing but the best for you!" she crooned to the quivering little blobs. Greg and I left for school, shocked and saddened by what we'd witnessed, keenly aware that our throats were naked and exposed to the winter wind, and hoping that somewhere, Kurt Waldheim was also cold and miserable, feeling shame over his ignominious dismissal, and wondering what had happened to his beloved scarf.

Later that afternoon as I trudged home from school with a chest full of phlegm, clutching my fashionable polyester jacket tight against the raw January sleet, I cursed the day those puppies were ever born. I devised a plan wherein I would steal the scarf away while Googie was at work and then, when she discovered the shivering newborns exposed to the elements, I would simply blame Greg. It was genius! I raced home, eager to feel the caress of cashmere once again, but was dismayed to find my grandmother still on the couch, watching over the box full of suckling pups.

"Why aren't you at work?" I asked, trying to sound casual as I eyeballed the puppies and the befouled and crusty scarf.

"I couldn't go because of this," she said, pointing to a small, squirming lump in her lap. "Gremlin took one of the puppies out of the box and dropped him in a corner. Isn't he adorable?"

I looked at the impossibly small creature my grandmother was hand feeding from the world's tiniest bottle. A little trickle of doggie formula pooled around the corners of his mouth.

"He would have died if I hadn't found him, poor baby. I'm going to stay home with him until he's strong enough to travel." Googie cradled him in her warm hands, and I felt a surge of guilt. What kind of monster was I, eager to steal the bedding away from helpless puppies, while my saintly grandmother sacrificed her time and energy for this poor, unfortunate reject?

"Well, he sure is cute. Can I help you care for him? Would you like me to wash that scarf maybe?" I said, but Googie wasn't really listening to me as she held the tiny puppy up to her lips and peppered him with grandmotherly kisses.

By the following week, Googie had decided that the puppy was strong enough to venture out and accompany her to work, despite the howling winds and frigid temperatures. She bundled herself up in her usual seven or eight layers of sensible clothing, packed the puppy in the Nazi scarf and nestled him carefully in her Channel Thirteen canvas tote, and waved to us cheerfully as she drove away in the Dart. Once at work, she devised a clever way to keep the puppy comfortable and warm and under her watchful eye: she nestled him snuggly in her ample cleavage with just his wee little head sticking out. Googie's coworkers quickly became accustomed to the sight of the puppy peeking out from his fleshy cradle, and even the most prominent Council members took time out of their busy days to express their good wishes to her. One such notable dignitary was Bishop Desmond Tutu, who, upon learning that my grandmother's charge was a cast out runt, blessed the puppy and commended Googie for her kind devotion to him. Without skipping a beat, my grandmother announced that she would name the puppy Bishop Desmond Tutu and vowed that she would cherish him to the end of his days. The human Bishop Tutu thanked my grandmother for the honor, while the squirming, mewling, newborn Bishop Tutu pooped in my grandmother's bra.

Later that afternoon, Googie was in a great rush to get home and announce to her family that the once rejected puppy she had saved from certain doom had been blessed by the world famous South African activist and humanitarian. She bundled herself up against the wintry elements and carried her precious cargo in his insulated canvas bag out to the car, loaded him in to the passenger side, along with all her various purses and totes, and promptly locked herself out. Googie soon attracted a crowd with her shrieks of "HELP ME! BISHOP DESMOND TUTU IS LOCKED IN MY CAR! HELP!" Throngs of passers-by stopped to look in the car, and were annoyed and disappointed to see no celebrity cleric freezing to death in the back seat, and simply moved on. But my grandmother's persistent screaming finally attracted a crowd and the attentions of a police officer, whose attempts to calm her down only added to her fear.

"What seems to be the problem, ma'am?"

"GET THAT DOOR OPEN! HE'S GOING TO FREEZE! OH GOD! HURRY!"

"Oh, 'he' is going to freeze, is he?" said the officer as he eyed the Channel Thirteen tote and the cracked brown leather handbag. "Let's just calm down for a minute..."

"NO NO NO! MY PRECIOUS BISHOP DESMOND TUTU IS IN THERE! HE'S IN THAT TOTE! OH GOD!"

The officer was about to call for an ambulance to cart my ranting grandmother off to a nice, warm hospital bed, when she finally calmed down enough to explain that Tutu was a tiny puppy who would not last much longer in the frozen car. The well-intended policeman struggled to get the door pried open, as Googie screamed in his ear "OH GOD! WHY ISN'T IT OPENING? OH GOD!" when, as luck would have it, a nice young man with a crowbar happened to be passing by, and seeing the distress my grandmother was in, offered to help. He swiftly jimmied the door open, much to Googie's enormous relief. He received a warm round of applause from the crowd, and a genuinely grateful hug from Googie. Even the police officer thanked him with a pat on the back.

"Wait, there was a 'nice, young man' with a crowbar walking down 5th Avenue on the upper east side?" I asked my grandmother later that night, as we sat around the dinner table. "Didn't anyone find that a little suspicious?"

"What do you mean? Weren't you listening? Don't you understand what happened, here? He saved my sweet precious Tutu! He appeared like a guardian angel!" Googie retold the story while nuzzling the puppy, and we let her enjoy the retelling by not mentioning the fact that a practiced car thief had aided in Tutu's rescue.

To no one's surprise, Tutu grew up to be a less than strapping young buck. For starters, he never left the safe confines of Googie's lap, which did nothing to improve his stunted, misshapen appearance. She carted him around with her from morning 'til night, only putting him down to use the bathroom, at which point he would hide under a couch cushion and growl at anyone that came near. We would attempt to lure him out with Milk Bones, but having been raised on a diet of poached breast of chicken and seared beef tenderloin, he naturally assumed we were trying to poison him, and he would lash out with his snaggled, malformed teeth. Even when secure within the folds of Googie's warm embrace, Tutu trusted no one, and we all suffered his lightning quick lunge for the jugular as we leaned in to kiss our grandmother goodnight. Part of the problem may have been that he just didn't see us due to the swath of hair growing over his left eyeball, while his right bulged unnervingly from its socket and gazed permanently towards Mecca. His protruding teeth prevented his mouth from closing properly, and he breathed in ragged gulps and wheezes. His back was hunched, his legs were too short, and his nails grew in crazy configurations. Googie was unfazed by Tutu's freakish malformations, and would lovingly gaze into his hairy eyeball while whispering sweet nothings into his stone deaf ears. The only time I ever saw Googie become alarmed was when she took him to the vet to be neutered, only to find that he, in fact, had no testicles.

"Oh my poor baby! How's this going to affect his health?" she asked the doctor with concern, as Tutu ran amok and attacked the doctor's assistant, slicing open her nose from bridge to tip.

"I think you've got nothing to worry about" the vet patiently reassured her, as he applied pressure to the young assistant's gaping wound with one hand and dialed 911 with the other.

"That doctor doesn't know anything!" my grandmother declared that evening, propping Tutu closer to her plate of pot roast. "It's obvious that my little darling needs medical intervention" she said, as Tutu wolfed down the pile of beef and potatoes in rich brown gravy. We tried to pay attention to the thread of the story, but found ourselves distracted by the sounds of Tutu snorting, growling and gasping his way through Googie's dinner.

"He looks ok to me," I offered, as I pushed my own plate away, having lost my appetite. "I mean, he doesn't look any worse than he usually looks."

Googie nibbled at the scraps of meat that Tutu had left behind. "How can you say that? Look at that face! I think he's beautiful. Don't you think he's beautiful?"

My brother and I turned away as Tutu gagged repeatedly on a stalk of celery, causing his bulging eye to teeter on the verge of ejection. "Sure!" we agreed, but Greg was trying to hide the fact that he had thrown up into his napkin.

In the end, Googie left well enough alone, leaving Tutu's raisin sized undescended testes to remain tucked up in his taint, where I imagined strange and twisted sperms bounced around in their tiny prison, frantically seeking release, causing Tutu to be in a perpetual state of angry confusion. Googie loved him unconditionally, despite the fact that he eventually failed to recognize her as the person who owned the lap he was so attached to, and he would randomly attack her without warning.

"Oh, he's just a little confused!" she would say, staunching the flow of blood with the hem of her dress. "I moved my hand when he wasn't ready, and it surprised him. For all he knew, I might have been a murderous assailant. Look, the bleeding's almost stopped! I don't even think it'll need stitches!" We begged Googie to put Tutu down once in a while, just to let the numerous festering wounds on her arms and neck begin to heal, but even the slightest attempt to relocate him would send Tutu into a snarling fit of rage. Googie would calm him down with some smoked salmon and beg his forgiveness.

"No, no. Mommy's darling will stay right here in mommy's lap. Don't listen to them. I know what's best for you" she would reassure him. Tutu's hairy eye would roll crazily in its socket, his lips pulled back in a demented smile, and he would give Googie a warning gargle that reprisal was imminent, which more often than not, she would choose to ignore.

"Oh, what's the big deal?" she would scoff, as we attempted to help her bandage up yet another flesh wound while keeping just out of Tutu's attack range. "It's not like I'm losing a limb for God's sake!" Tutu would snap angrily at empty air, and then lick another morsel of smoked fish off of Googie's plate. "See? He's just hungry! I'd be angry too if I was hungry!"

There was no reasoning with Googie, even after Tutu became so confused that he lost the ability to distinguish between potential assassins and the lovingly prepared meals that she provided for him. Plate after plate of Googie's best dishes went crashing to the floor as Tutu defended himself against the likes of chicken liver pate and hand rolled meatballs. "I think he's just bored. Nobody likes to eat the same thing every day!" was Googie's explanation for Tutu's bizarre behavior as she mopped up the shattered remains of Coq au Vin and Wedgewood China. Despite his full on war against humanity and foodstuffs, Tutu managed to remain relatively healthy and full of rage for years to come. That is, until his confusion finally led him to mistrust even his own body parts and he began attacking himself with wild abandon. My grandmother tried swaddling him like a newborn babe to protect him from his own razor sharp teeth, but every evening after she'd gone to bed, Tutu would wrestle himself out of his cotton prison and let loose his fury on whatever limb happened to be in his field of hairy vision. Tutu eventually lost, or possibly won, the war against himself, and Ernie buried him beneath his wild rose bush in the backyard, which, the following year, produced hard brownish lumps in place of the usual pale pink rosebuds. Ernie attempted to prune away the stunted, unattractive nuggets, but the bush retaliated by growing in unmanageable tangles covered in vicious thorns that left infected welts on Ernie's unprotected hands and arms. Googie nearly killed my grandfather when she caught him going at the rosebush with a hacksaw, and Ernie knew to leave well enough alone. The rosebush never again grew those lovely pink flowers, but every summer, when the crusty brown pods began popping out all over the bush's well armed branches, my grandmother would don her oven mitts and, ever so carefully, snip herself a strange bouquet, which she would place in her Depression era green glass vase and display it on the dining room table for all to admire.

"So beautiful", she would say, lovingly arranging the unruly and dangerous mess. "Don't you think they're beautiful?"

Bishop Desmond Tutu, the Runt of the Litter

My Better Half

My mother sat Buddha style in the center of her caved in bed, 32-ounce plastic tumbler of Colt 45 in one hand and a fresh, unwrapped pack of Marlboros in the other. I sat across from her on an ancient high back chair that had splintered arm rests and no stuffing left in the seat cushion, save for some filthy fluff that clung to the busted zipper. I'd passed up an entertaining afternoon of hanging out and smoking cigarettes on the stoop with my friends to spend what I hoped would be quality time with my mother. The mood was contemplative as we sat there, the two of us, in her tiny basement apartment. The TV was on, and her favorite soap, General Hospital, was starting, but something I had just said was distracting her and she was only half paying attention. A disintegrating birth certificate lay open on my lap, and I tapped my fingers impatiently on my leg.

"So?" I said.

"Yeah, yeah, I'm thinking" my mother replied. I knew my question had taken her by surprise, and now she was stalling as she stacked the new pack of smokes and her trusty Bic lighter on the milk crate night stand, right next to her plastic rosary and a framed picture of Lenny Bruce. She made a show of picking through the contents of the ceramic frog ashtray, and finally came up with a used, slightly squashed smokeable butt. She smoothed it out, and then carefully, so as not to set her own hair on fire, tilted her head to one side, torched the end and inhaled.

"Ok, what do you want to know?" she asked. She flicked nervously at the cigarette, the acrid stink of burning filter already filling the room. She took another drag anyway and then crushed it back out in the frog belly.

"Is Max my father or not?" I repeated.

My mother winced as she searched for another used smoke, but her expression was giving nothing away.

"Do you want him to be?" She deftly threw the bomb back in my own lap, and for a brief moment I thought about the man I was raised to believe was my father, the man whose name was right there on my birth certificate. This question, although irrelevant to the actual issue of paternity, gave me a wonderful if fleeting sense of control, and I held the tattered document up, reexamining the space labeled FATHER as if some new revelation might appear.

Countless times I had taken that birth certificate out of the yellowed envelope and carefully unfolded it, examining it for that smoking gun, but all I ever got was a vague sense of uneasiness, of something being not quite right. Nestled in beside the document was the only existing photograph of the two of them, a faded Polaroid of Max, decked out in his Army uniform arm in arm with my mother, who was looking uncomfortable in a frumpy department store dress and Go-Go boots. They were posing for the camera on the front steps of Town Hall, where they had just tied the knot in a civil ceremony. Someone had scribbled in ball point pen, "Max and Judi, 1964" across the white strip at the bottom of the picture, where there was still plenty of space to mark down the nature of the occasion, or even the actual date, but no one had bothered. I would stare at that picture for hours, searching Max's face for any hint of something familiar, something I could connect to my own face, like the slant of my eyes or the upward slope of my nose, but I couldn't find anything. If the birth certificate was correct he was all of eighteen and she was twenty-three, which meant I was five years old at the time of their nuptials. If Max really was my father, he would have been thirteen when I was conceived. I wondered if that was even possible, shuddering at the thought and hoping maybe the birth certificate was wrong. And where was I during this momentous occasion? Wasn't I invited? Was I sharing a bar stool with my grandfather at the Gin Mill, while my mother and Max, a young man barely out of high school, stood before a judge and pledged their eternal devotion to each other? The two of them looked distractedly at the photographer, my mother's cheap bouquet of white chrysanthemums the only give-away that a marriage had taken place. Max posed stiffly, awkwardly, his left arm pinning my mother's right to his side, forcing a smile that contorted the left side of his face. The viewer might wonder, what's going on here? The slouching young woman wearing the bargain-basement dress and too much black eye liner appears bored and out of place hanging on the arm of the young man in uniform, who looks as if he may be having a stroke. I knew nothing about how these two young lovers had met, what fateful event had brought them together. My mother was always eager to share stories of her misspent youth, but Max never played a part in any of them. I'd heard the wild tales of her beatnik days hanging out in Village coffee houses with dangerous bongo playing boyfriends, of how she repeatedly ran away from home to live in Washington Square Park to eat out of dumpsters and pee behind cars until my grandfather hunted her down and ferried her back uptown to the Bronx. She especially loved recounting tales of her time in the Green Meadows Home for Unwed Mothers, which is where my grandparents put her the last time they dragged her home kicking, screaming and filthy in torn capri pants and a too-tight black turtle neck that barely covered the baby bulge. Green Meadows was a secluded facility somewhere near the Hunt's Point fish market in the south Bronx, where the teen residents served their time hidden behind barred windows and dormitory doors that locked from the outside. Having safely stowed their bad girls away from the judgmental stares of friends and neighbors, mortified parents were free to invent stories of private colleges, trips abroad or visits to long lost relatives on the West Coast. The girls would spend the better part of their nine-month tenure diapering baby dolls and throwing up, which was not so much from the pregnancy hormones as from the constant stench of the fish market that wafted in through the barred windows on the river breeze. Green Meadows was a rough place, and my mother was proud to say that she never once got beat up there, thanks to her bunk mate Carla, a tough girl from Arthur Avenue who boasted that she got knocked up by one of the Fordham Baldies. Carla often confided in my mother about her gang-related escapades, and confessed that she was having a hard time figuring out who the father was.

"It mighta been Tony Two Toes 'cause we did it standin' up, but Frankie Mozzarella has a bigger dick, so I'm thinkin' it mighta been him, ya know?" Carla worried that the baby would be born in sin, and she wanted the real father to pay for a big, fancy baptismal party. "This way God won't think I'm no dead beat," she explained. My mother assured her that given the undeniable scientific evidence, Frankie Mozzarella had to be the father, and he should not only pay for the baptism but also prove his love for Carla by getting her a great big diamond engagement ring and a sack of White Castle burgers, which my mother had been craving since being forced to eat institutional food, which made her vomit with even more frequency than usual. Carla was so thrilled and grateful to have a solution to her quandary that, after phoning the father-to-be and demanding delivery of a ring along with twenty-five Murder Burgers, she stabbed one of the dormitory matrons who had locked my mother in her room for a whole day when she refused to eat her spaghetti. "You know me," my mother had said by way of an explanation, "I can't eat spaghetti unless it's al dente!" Although Carla and my mother went their separate ways, they vowed to stay in touch. My mother saved all the letters that Carla sent her from Riker's Island, and sometimes we would read them together and laugh at all the ways Carla managed to get herself into trouble.

As entertaining as these stories were, I always knew something was amiss. Where did Max fit in to this picture? Amid all the wacky tales of misconduct and impregnation, there was a distinct absence of the man who planted the seed. I longed to make sense of it all. I tried to put Max into my memories alongside my mother and grandparents, but all I could remember was that almost immediately after that wedding picture was taken, Max was stationed overseas. "Daddy's gone to Germany!" my mother proudly informed me, and I couldn't help but assume that "daddy" had been there all along, and I simply hadn't been paying attention. In an apparent effort to prove herself marriage-worthy and capable of normality, my mother went through a major transformation and tossed out all her hipster clothing, cut her hair into a neat bob, and even ditched her beloved black eye liner. The hours she used to spend listening to Miles and Coltrane she now spent pouring over her brand new collection of Betty Crocker's "Great Meals in 15 Minutes!" She and I would gather fall leaves to send to Max in a big manila envelope along with notes of love and longing. At my mother's prompting I would write "I love you, daddy!" and draw a little stick figure family, with my mother sporting the giant baby belly that would soon become my brother. It was quite the romantic scenario, the pregnant, dutiful wife and her little girl, eagerly awaiting the hero dad's return. When Max came home the following spring, Greg was already born and my mother, bored to death of hand washing diapers and living under my grandparents' roof in suburban Long Island, was happy to follow Max wherever the army decided to send him, perhaps envisioning herself living the high life in Chicago or St. Louis, or better yet, San Francisco, where the new free love movement appealed to her latent subversive tendencies. To this end, she grew out her hair and bought herself another black eye liner and a pair of hip hugging bell bottoms, but much to her dismay, Max was told to report for duty to some sleepy little town on the outskirts of Providence, Rhode Island. We moved into an enormous, dilapidated seaside Victorian, where her wildest diversion was beating the salt crystals out of Greg's frozen, line-dried diapers. At first, Max made an effort to come home for dinner on a fairly regular basis, and for a short time we all acted like one big, happy family, but my mother, limited by the meager army stipend and unable to grasp the concept of a well-balanced meal, took to frying up plate loads of Spam every night, and before long Max wearied of canned meat products and found excuses to stay at the barracks. Out of lonely desperation, my mother attempted to make friends with the live-in landlady, an angry, mistrustful Haitian woman, named Carolina, who made it abundantly clear that she not only hated my mother, but that all white people were devils not to be trusted. Carolina would often sit in the front parlor on a faded, fraying settee reading her bible and making little dolls out of straw, and what appeared to be real human hair. My mother would approach her with a heaping plate of leftover fried Spam and try striking up conversation.

"So, Carolina! I see you have a real talent for the Arts and Crafts!"

"Wachoo tink I gonna do? Eat dat devil poison? Jesus gonna make you pay, you see!" and Carolina would spit right on her own thread bare rug and stuff another wad of hair into a doll that bore an uncanny resemblance to my mother. Sometimes out of crushing boredom, we would all venture out into the frigid Rhode Island wind. While we were gone, Carolina would perch herself at the top of the grand, sweeping staircase that led up to our second-floor apartment, arms folded, a joyless smile stretched over her pearly-white, perfect teeth, waiting patiently for us to come in from dragging Greg's carriage through the cold, muddy sand. My mother would return home chilled to the bone, nose running, hands frozen onto the carriage handle, and Carolina would silently watch her struggle up the stairs, Greg's bald head bouncing each time the wheels thumped up another step. "Hi, Carolina!" my mother would call cheerfully over her shoulder, terrified that Carolina would plant a foot in her back and send her careening head first to her death, with little baby Greg not far behind. Once at the top step, gasping and breathless, my mother would murmur some pleasantries and avoid eye contact with Carolina, who cursed her with Patois invectives, repeatedly spitting in my mother's wake as she beat a hasty retreat to the drafty apartment.

When she wasn't busy gaslighting my mother, Carolina would prowl the sprawling estate and its acres of chilly, damp, beach-front property, with a well-worn leather belt in hand in search of her ne'er do well twin teenage daughters. Jinkin and Jody made it their daily mission to evade their mother, and find clever and creative ways to enjoy cigarettes, jug wine and boys without their belt-wielding mother ever finding out. The old house lent itself perfectly to this mission, and the girls utilized every trap door, back stair and crawlspace to carry out their illicit activities. Every once in a while, though, Carolina would sniff them out and they would show up at our door, scratching furtively and begging to be let in, the ever diligent Carolina and her trusty belt not far behind, vowing to bring down the wrath of God on their heathen heads if she caught them drinking that devil's brew. My mother was terrified that Carolina would find her girls hiding in our tiny apartment, but the need for some companionship and debauchery outweighed her fear and the three of them would pass around the jug and play five card stud for cigarettes until the wee hours of the morning, when Carolina would finally quit her prowling. The twins would then quietly slip out the door and tip toe down the long, dark hallway, past their mother's bedroom, where she could be heard wailing and praying at the top of her lungs until the sun came up.

"Oh Jesus! Why you do dis to me? Why you bring dis white devil to me? Why? Why?"

My mother suspected that Carolina knew what was going on, and the day she found one of those creepy straw dolls pinned to our apartment door by its head, she packed up our things and we headed home to New York.

I was thinking about Max and that dreary year we spent in Rhode Island as I absentmindedly picked at the splinters on the armrest, waiting for further clarification from my mother. My memories of that time had a washed out, ghostly quality, like a movie shot in black and white through a lens coated with Vaseline. I remember feeling scared and lonely in that big house, petrified of Carolina and her thinly-veiled animosity, and overwhelmed by shyness around Max on the rare occasions when he would show up. I tried to picture his face, but all I could come up with was that image from the wedding photo. I had no memories of school or friends or anything outside of the peeling, cheerless house on the beach, and I never even questioned why, after we moved back to New York, Max seemingly disappeared into thin air. In my mind the transition was seamless. One minute, Max and my mother are holding my hands as I stand knee-deep in the icy New England surf, and the next, we are living back on Long Island; my mother, brother and I, in a house perched on the edge of the Grumman's Airfield, where the roar of planes taking off and landing was so constant that it was practically unnoticeable, like the sound of your own heartbeat. My mother never offered an explanation. Max was gone and it didn't matter one way or the other whether he was around or not. I was seven years old at the time, and now here I was, eight years later, wondering why I hadn't questioned these gaps in the story before.

I watched my mother digging through the frog belly, but this time all she could find were burnt filters, and she finally resorted to opening the new pack. I was hopeful that this was a sign that she was about to say something of great importance. She lit one up and pretended to be interested in General Hospital, but she was jiggling nervously. I glanced back down at the birth certificate, a photocopy that had been folded and refolded so many times that the creases were obscuring the print. I kept staring at the typed in words in the space labeled "FATHER: MAXWELL LEVINE," by now just a meaningless sequence of letters.

"You were supposed to be put up for adoption, you know" my mother blurted out suddenly, not exactly the revelation I'd been sitting there waiting for, having heard this always entertaining tale dozens of times before. It was one of her favorite stories, and she would describe with great relish the day of my birth, the long hours of waiting, the pain, the pushing, the vomiting, the blood and gore and screaming, followed by the usual complaints regarding institutional food and unattractive hospital gowns, and ultimately, how I was spared being given away to strangers thanks to my grandparents, who apparently were making all the decisions. Never was there a mention of Max, or any other guy for that matter, nor of any overwhelming maternal urges on my mother's part, but none of that mattered. What mattered was that she cursed out the doctor and threw a bedpan at his head when he refused to give her any pain-killing drugs, and kicked her labor nurse in the face as she tried to cross my mothers' legs as I began to crown on the way to the delivery room. I was thrilled that I had a starring role in this tale, that in fact it was sheer adorableness on my part that had them tearing up those adoption papers, which is why I got to go home with my underage mother to the tiny Levittown house where I would be raised more or less by my doting grandparents, while my mother resumed her care free life of sleeping the days away and hitchhiking rides to The Village at night.

I reflected on my mother's attempt to distract me from the real topic at hand and wondered why, after unabashedly sharing all the other sordid details of her rebellious life, she was avoiding this one. I thought about our time spent living on the edge of the airfield, where she met a tough-talking Italian guy from the Bronx. His name was Tony but everybody called him Batman, and my mother fell hard for him in spite of the fact that he wore a trench coat and slacks. Something about their chemistry was destructive and volatile, but I never saw my mother as happy as when she was with him. His visits to our noisy apartment were always brief, and afterwards she would cry and break things and yell, knowing he was going home to his wife and kids. Once again, the man in my mothers' life was barely there, and this seemed perfectly normal to me. I was confused about my mother's erratic behavior when she was with Batman, but knowing next to nothing about the mysterious world of grown-ups, I assumed that all of them cried for hours and resorted to blowing their noses into socks after all the toilet paper got used up.

I looked over at my mother now, as she stubbed out her cigarette, while there was still plenty of good tobacco left in it, planning ahead for the lean times in case there was no new pack in the near future. I hadn't bothered responding to her less than earth-shattering adoption revelation, and apparently she wasn't expecting me to as she drained the last drop from her tumbler of beer, and then leaned over to lower the volume on the TV set. "I'm gonna take a nap" she announced, and curled herself up in the permanent hollow of the broken bed.

I sat there fuming in the high-back chair, knowing it would be futile to pursue any further discussion. The birth certificate, damp from my sweaty hands, lay across my lap and at that moment, I hated my mother for denying me the chance to decipher its mysteries. I imagined how satisfying it would be to just tear the thing up into tiny pieces, or reach over and grab the Bic lighter and set it and that infuriating photograph ablaze, and watch as their pretend smiles went up in flames. For a while, I just sat there staring at the flickering images on the TV, occasionally glancing at my mother as she slept, her long, bony legs pulled up tight, mouth slightly agape. Even in slumber, her face was hard and angular, so unlike my own. I pulled the photograph out of the envelope and examined it for the thousandth time and then propped it up on the milk crate nightstand against the ceramic frog ashtray and, refolding the birth certificate, I placed it back in the envelope. I checked to make sure my mother was really asleep before I got up and went to the cabinet where she kept an old jewelry box full of relics from her hippie days. Opening it, I reached in to pull out a fistful of love beads when I caught my reflection in the mirror inside, partially obscured by the tiny plastic ballerina that twirled whenever the top was up. I pushed the ballerina down with my finger to get a better look at myself, and turning my face to a three quarter angle, I forced a smile and noticed something strangely familiar. It was nothing specific, nothing I recognized at first, until I realized with a start it was unmistakably my mother. I looked away, unsure how to feel about this, and then looking back I saw her again, in my smile, my chin, even the tilt of my head. I quickly averted my eyes, wondering why I never noticed it before. I let the little ballerina spring back into place, and deliberately avoiding my reflection, I stuffed the envelope under the tangle of necklaces, closed the lid of the jewelry box and slid it back onto the shelf behind a pile of paperback books. I looked again at my mother who was snoring gently now, deep in a beer slumber and missing her favorite game show. She would undoubtedly sleep right through The Price Is Right, but I left the TV on to bathe her in the happy light of silently screaming ecstatic contestants and headed outside to find my friends.

Made in the USA
Charleston, SC
27 June 2014